CON B

BRINA SVIT was born in Slovenia between Paris and Slovenia. She works as a journalist, screenwriter and director, and has written three novels. *Con Brio* is her first novel to be translated into English.

PETER CONSTANTINE translates from many languages, including Albanian, Greek and Russian. He has written books on the languages and cultures of the Far East. His translation of *Six Early Stories* by Thomas Mann won the Pen/Book of the Month Club Translation Prize, and he won the National Translation Award for *The Undiscovered Chekhov*.

Also by Brina Svit

Fiction

APRIL

THE DEATH OF A SLOVENIAN PRIMA DONNA

Non-fiction

ORDINARY RELATIONSHIPS

(Co-written with Peter Kolšek)

Brina Svit

CON BRIO

Translated from the Slovenian by
Peter Constantine

THE HARVILL PRESS
LONDON

First published by Nova Revija, Slovenia, 1998
2 4 6 8 10 9 7 5 3 1
Copyright © Brina Svit, 1998 and © Editions Gallimard, 1999
English translation copyright © Peter Constantine, 2002

Brina Svit has asserted her right under the Copyright, Designs and Patents Act 1988 to be identified as the author of this work

This book is sold subject to the condition that it shall not, by way of trade or otherwise, be lent, resold, hired out, or otherwise circulated without the publisher's prior consent in any form of binding or cover other than that in which it is published and without a similar condition including this condition being imposed on the subsequent purchaser

First published in Great Britain in 2002 by
The Harvill Press
Random House, 20 Vauxhall Bridge Road,
London SW1V 2SA

Random House Australia (Pty) Limited
20 Alfred Street, Milsons Point, Sydney,
New South Wales 2061, Australia

Random House New Zealand Limited
18 Poland Road, Glenfield,
Auckland 10, New Zealand

Random House South Africa (Pty) Limited
Endulini, 5A Jubilee Road, Parktown 2193, South Africa

The Random House Group Limited Reg. No. 954009
www.randomhouse.co.uk

A CIP catalogue record for this book
is available from the British Library

ISBN 1 86046 857 8

Papers used by Random House are natural, recyclable products made from wood grown in sustainable forests; the manufacturing processes conform to the environmental regulations of the country of origin

Designed and typeset in Galliard by Libanus Press, Marlborough, Wiltshire

Printed and bound in Great Britain by
Biddles Ltd, Guildford and King's Lynn

CON BRIO

I

Early this morning I lit a cigarette – the only cigarette I can smoke with some pleasure and that at least has the power to halt time, to separate night from day, giving the impression that life is not simply an uninterrupted straight line – so, having lit this first cigarette of the day after a sleepless night, and after calling Ema, I suddenly thought how I wished I could write for the cinema.

For if I could write for the cinema, I realized in the sudden clarity of the morning cigarette's haze, I would write our story in a sequence of images, only modifying the dialogue a little.

The first images, the ones that come before the initial credits, before the title and the name of the screenwriter, the images that give the still screen an illusion of life, would be images of her hands. Hands resting on the second-to-last table in the back room of a restaurant I used to go to, not far from the boulevard Saint-Germain. The slim, delicate hands of a woman, hands that at first glance are almost forlorn, frail, and yet strong, with solid wrists that one can imagine gripping taut reins. Hands with long, flexible fingers and richly curved palms. And with round nails, gently cut as if still touched by childhood.

But all this, the tenderness and power in these hands, their readiness to act and their lingering childhood, one sees only later when they begin to move. When the waiter clears away the plates of our main course, creating a space between us. When we order ice cream and the waiter pours white wine into our glasses. And above all when I hear my voice, like that of someone speaking in my place, asking her, Katarina, Kati, slowly and distinctly, for her hand in marriage, asking her to come live with me in the rue Balzac. For a split second, she looks at me as if she were standing on the edge of a precipice. Then she glances at the table, and suddenly her hand reaches for the piece of paper that the waiter had slid under the edge of the tablecloth. She presses it between her palms, smoothes it out, and then begins folding it with her nimble, skilful fingers. I think I might want to add something or other here, perhaps how pleasant it is to be so close to her face, and how her radiance makes me think of flowing honey. But my eyes and thoughts cannot tear themselves away from her nimble hands, folding with total seriousness and concentration the bill that is covered with scribbles. She, too, is absorbed in her hands, as if they were not hers, or rather as if the connection between herself and her hands was more complex than was obvious at first glance. Later, I often thought that contrary to the saying, the entrance to *her* soul is not through her eyes, but her hands. These two delicate, living things that turned our restaurant bill into a sailboat a few centimetres long. She places the paper boat on her open palm, studies it from all sides, adjusts the sail one last time, grasps the boat between thumb and index finger, and cautiously, very cautiously, places it on the surface of the wine in her glass.

It is only now that she raises her eyes to me. There is not a trace of the surprise or fear that were in her face only a few seconds ago. Her expression is once more clear and open. Again I think I might want to add something, perhaps that I had never imagined, ever, that our lunch would take such a turn, that I had not even thought that she would come, and now that she is here, that she is sitting here in front of me, suddenly everything is different. And again I say nothing, for, the instant I open my mouth, she bends over her wineglass and moves her finger towards the sailboat. She taps the sail, pushing it to the opposite shore. The sail shivers and yields to the current.

Then she looks at me again and says, firmly, "Fine."

2

But for quite some time now Ema has no longer been here and, to be honest, I have never written for the cinema, nor had such an idea ever crossed my mind until this morning, even though my novel *Late Strawberries* was turned into a moderately successful film with the title *Late Love*, and even though Farkas has sold the film rights of other novels I have written, among them *The New New Héloïse*, about which a young filmmaker came to see me a year or so ago. He sat in the armchair facing the fireplace. Ema brought him a cup of coffee, which he set clumsily down between the legs of the armchair and promptly forgot. The floor seemed to be shaking under his feet, but he struggled to appear calm, nonchalant. I noticed that he had chewed his fingernails to the quick, that his high, glistening forehead was lengthened by a starkly receding hairline, and that his eyes were frightened, like those of a young fawn. In a single, drawn-out tirade, he explained that he had three problems with my novel, for which he had the highest regard: its pessimism, its clarity, and its rejection of love, which were all, unfortunately, elements incompatible with contemporary cinema, which strives to be optimistic, entertaining, and above all to believe in love, if you see what I mean. He looked at me with his fawn-like eyes. "And time, which you manage to wind like a thread around your finger with such ease, that renowned sense of time you have . . . But what a film needs, if you see what I mean, is definitive sharpness, because time in a film is basically always the present, and this is precisely how film differs from literature, which can easily afford to dart all over the place." This was why he intended to rearrange my plot – that is to say, if I agreed, if I did not mind – so that the film would begin where it ought to begin, and end where it ought to end.

I did not mind, everything he said was clear as spring water, and as I bade him farewell at the door, I murmured that he could do as he pleased, that he was right, that it was perfectly fine with me. He ran his hand over his receding hair and looked at me with moist gratitude. As I took his undrunk coffee back to the kitchen, it struck me for the first time that my books – fortunately for me, and unfortunately for Farkas – were completely uncinematographic. No one could turn their pessimism into optimism, their doubt into certainty, their lack of faith into faith. No one could butcher them, deciding where they should begin and where they should end. And until this morning, the screenwriter's visit had been the last time I had given any thought to what people call the "seventh art".

So if I did know how to write in the eternal, obsessive present of the cinema, leaving aside the question of benevolent sentiments, I would begin in the back room of a boulevard Saint-Germain restaurant which I do not intend to name.

Which I do not intend to name because I do not wish to divulge the name of its owner, and because I would prefer that that little corner, that table, that place in the heart of Paris, which witnessed such momentous changes in our lives, remain ours alone. If I did know how to write screenplays that had the power to enthral the viewer from the very first moment, I would begin with her hands, the paper sailboat rocking on the white Burgundy, and her cool voice, answering an elderly gentleman with greying hair and faded eyes who asked her for her hand in marriage, firmly saying "Fine".

But since I cannot (to stress this one last time) and do not intend to write for the cinema, possibly because I cannot subjugate the eternal present, I will attempt to describe what happened to us, the way I always have: in a book. And I will not attempt to modify the dialogue, even though I would like to. Not even the most crucial dialogues. The ones that have made things the way they are between us, turning us into one of the most unusual couples in this city. And when I say "unusual", I know whereof I speak.

3

We met at Farkas's place.

"Tibor, you son of a lion! Will you do me a favour?" he had said to me that morning over the phone.

Not again, I thought. Of all the people I know, Farkas is the man with the toughest hide. How many times had I told him that I detested that phrase, and even more than the phrase, that sub-Danubian, sub-Carpathian undertone with which he has pronounced it for a good twenty-five years. And not only the phrase "son of a lion", which he keeps calling me in front of everybody.

"I cannot come," I interrupted him, and began listing the engagements that I might well have had: Simon Osterman's concert, dinner with Baleli, a slight headache, a radio interview.

"I've had your interview moved to next week," he said, interrupting me in turn. "Simon Osterman is on tour in Italy, there's a bottle of aspirin in your kitchen in the third drawer from the top, and Baleli is one of the most understanding women in the world, at any rate the type of woman who understands that from time to time one has to rush off to help someone in need, to be available, to be at someone's disposal, to be on hand for instance to help a young author, a babe in the woods if you will, though not wholly uninteresting, who has written a first novel for which we need to generate some attention, some interest . . . I've just published him. But one thing I'd dearly like to know is what you're up to every evening."

To be at someone's disposal, to be on hand, to rush off to help someone in need, what I'm up to every evening . . . Absolutely nothing, I murmured to myself as I chose a shirt, a jacket, and a pair of good shoes, deciding to walk to Farkas's place and have a drink or two with the promising author whose first novel, according to Farkas, was unreadable, even though this fellow does seem to have something. Absolutely nothing, a big, ponderous, practically immobile nothing . . . time that flows evenly like blood from a body . . .

The sky above the rue Balzac was resplendent as it hadn't been for a long time, though the aroma of imminent rain hung in the air. On the avenue de Friedland, practically empty at this hour, a tramp grinned at me. I walked on a few paces, but then went back to the antique shop with the Venetian lamps in front of which he was sitting. Two small, pale-green eyes peered out from his bloated, grey face, as if they were lying in wait. He recognized me before I even opened my mouth, and grinned at me again, this time in a friendlier way. I bought a pack of cigarettes in a café at the corner of the rue Bonaparte and entered the courtyard where, above the door of a narrow, two-storey building with heavily flaking plaster, in gold letters, were the words: Editions F. Farkas.

The second floor was brightly lit, and on the stairs I could hear the sounds of people at a cocktail party. A young man in livery standing by the door – Farkas obviously had faith in the future of his new author – smiled at me obsequiously as he tried to take my coat. I refused with a curt wave, and went in. "Hmm, hmm," I muttered, eyeing the crowd, which had been selected with more than usual care, the dresses cut lower, a few carefully chosen, exotic guests sprinkled here and there. It made me think of a courtyard filled with exquisite fowl (myself included) and a few aristocratic cockerels. Farkas was obviously up to something. I mingled. After all, I have always followed the rules of the game. I was handed a glass of champagne. The flash of a camera blinded me for an instant. Farkas nodded at me from across the room. After thirty years of being immersed in Paris, I thought, as I always did on such occasions, he still hadn't learned how to hide his sub-Carpathian nature. It is easy to recognize Farkas in a crowd: a boisterous, spluttering laugh, an unerring bad taste in clothes, and a pencil moustache that only he would dare sport. A young couple stood next to him: a man wearing eccentric glasses and a small redhead with a feather boa draped over her shoulders. If that fellow with the glasses was the new, up-and-coming author, I said to myself, then his "something", judging from Farkas's expression, was hidden behind those ivory-rimmed lenses. I made my way to the buffet, nodding at a familiar face and managing to shake off a woman who was clinging to me as if her life depended on it. I eyed the dishes approvingly, because when it came to food and drink, you could trust Farkas implicitly. I poured myself another glass of champagne and thought of the tramp beneath the Venetian lamps. A guitar was playing in the background.

It was during the first Andalusian chords, at least that's how I remember it today, that I heard someone coughing behind me. Coughing, wheezing, spluttering. I turned around and saw a woman's back, doubled over in spasms. I slapped it. Once, twice, three times. The back bent lower beneath my slaps. My hand became entangled in her long hair. I slapped her back again, and then once more, just below the nape of her neck. The back began to calm down, raise itself, straighten up. It took a few deep breaths and turned. I looked into a wet, smudged face that was smiling at me through tears. The young, blonde woman nodded her thanks at me as she wiped her smeared cheeks. I took a well-pressed handkerchief from my pocket and held it out to her. She burst out laughing, as if I had just done the most inappropriate thing in the world. I put the handkerchief back in my pocket and shrugged my shoulders. I cannot say that she made any particular impression on me. She was a blonde, a real one, I suppose, and except for her short, green, sleeveless dress, which at first glance I took for a Peter Pan outfit, and the string of genuine dark pearls around her neck, she looked like any woman one might encounter at a cocktail party.

And yet I was rather pleased that something had lodged itself in her throat and that I had happened to be standing in front of her, and not in front of the promising young man with the spectacles, in front of his feather boa, or any other similar specimens who were waiting more or less patiently for their big moment. And when she gave me her hand, saying she was leaving, I murmured, "Me too, me too," and followed in her wake. Before we reached the door I looked around the room one last time for Farkas. He was still standing next to the bespectacled man and the feather boa, but he turned and looked at us. I nodded to him and waited a moment for him to nod back. God knows what he was thinking, and why a pensive smile, if it was a smile, had spread over his face. I nodded once more and left the cocktail party. I was again blinded by the flash of a camera. The man in livery at the door handed her her coat – a short, funny thing made of black velvet with innumerable buttons. He helped her into it. She slowly slipped on her long black gloves, which struck me, and clearly the liveried man too, as primarily a dressing ritual – especially in mid-April which, despite its whimsical weather, was not particularly cold. We walked down the stairs, crossed the courtyard, and plunged into the April night.

4

“Few species can survive outside of any kind of collective life: leopards, martens, squirrels, badgers, and . . . me.” I had first told Baleli this when we had breakfast on the day of our divorce, now some twenty-eight years ago, and had then repeated the phrase quite often on all kinds of occasions. I think I even jotted it down somewhere, adding badgers, and Benz, my vagabond of a cat, while Simon Osterman quite openly appropriated it (in a version that went: “squirrels, badgers, R. A. Tibor, and me”). I still do not know why I repeated this list of animals, a list I had no doubt taken to heart because of its resonant quality, this evening of all evenings, as we walked down the rue Bonaparte away from Farkas, releasing ourselves into the night. Leopards, martens, squirrels, badgers, Benz, and me.

The evening had lost its sumptuous quality, and it had begun to rain. We walked side by side without saying a word, without even trying to say a word.

The rain started falling finer and harder, and I asked her where she lived. She stopped for a moment, looked at me in surprise, and standing on tiptoe pointed into the distance. I nodded, and stopped the first taxi that came along. We sat next to each other, and when the driver turned to me, I only pointed into the distance, beyond the Seine, as she had done. The driver, a large-framed Arab, shrugged his shoulders and set off. He must have taken us for ignorant tourists or foreigners lost in the metropolis.

I leaned back on the seat and reflected that the evening

had taken a completely unexpected turn, something that hadn't happened to me in a long time. Here I was sitting next to a young woman I did not know, having saved her air passages from something or other, and was taking her home, to a destination I did not know, somewhere in the north of town. Fortunately for me, the young woman was not talkative. I have always liked to sit silently in taxis, letting my thoughts roam free. She too had settled herself comfortably on the seat, had laid her gloved hands on her knees, and was staring forward into the darkness and the rain pounding the windscreen. And suddenly I wanted us to go on riding this way, next to each other behind the Arab's broad shoulders, in this silence disturbed only by the swishing of the windshield wipers and the faraway noise of the city. Leopards, martens, squirrels, badgers, Benz, and . . . me. The phrase was perhaps not even mine. I had most likely read it somewhere and had appropriated it during the breakfast with Baleli on the day of our divorce, though I had probably changed the order. Leopards, martens, squirrels . . . I almost always blindly follow my ear for language, which even Simon Osterman calls infallible.

"Stop over there," she said, again pointing somewhere in front of her.

The driver mumbled something into his beard, and slammed on the brakes in front of the brightly lit display window of a pharmacy with a flickering green cross above it.

So here we are, I said to myself, and turned to her. She began taking off her gloves. Shafts of green light flickered coldly over her face. I suddenly realized that she would give me her hand, thank me for the ride, open the door, and disappear for ever into the darkness.

"May I invite you for lunch?" I said, as if I had suddenly woken up.

"Lunch?" she asked, drawing out the word unnaturally, smiling at me.

"What is your name?" I asked her.

"Grushenka."

It was only now that I really heard her voice. Simon Osterman would have termed it a "lyric mezzo", a Michaela, an Octavian, a Delilah, a Carmen. What came to my mind was that she, too, was not French. Not because of her name – I had met quite a few Ivans, Mityas, and Alyoshas in Paris – but because of the accent she placed on the first syllable, because of the "a", which was dark and deep, and half-expired in her throat. The French never let a final syllable expire in their throats. I looked out the window at the house number over the door. Seventeen.

"Katarina," I said, turning towards her.

"Grushenka," she corrected me.

"Kati," I continued, taken aback that after such a long time I was again in the grip of my "renaming illness", as Baleli called that obsession which I had first applied to myself, and then had continued with others, particularly women. "Kati, tomorrow at one, at a restaurant called . . ."

"I can't tomorrow," she interrupted me, pulling her hair back behind her ears.

"How about the day after tomorrow, at one o'clock, no, let's make it half past one," I persisted with easy nonchalance.

She looked down at the floor, as if she had lost something or was eyeing her shoes. The driver slumped back in his seat and heaved a deep sigh. She quickly sat up, took hold of her gloves, and for an instant laid her hand on my knee.

"The day after tomorrow then," she said, got out, waved goodbye with her gloves, and slammed the car door shut. The driver and I watched her go, not into number seventeen next to the pharmacy, but along the boulevard with its plantain trees, stopping to light a cigarette, then disappearing. Leopards, martens, squirrels, badgers . . . and . . .

5

With the years a layer of order and discipline had settled around me. When I began to realize that I was waking up more or less at the same time every day, that I ate my unvarying breakfast exactly half an hour later, that I began dictating at nine and continued dictating (taking only a short break here and there) until one, when Marie-Hélène would lower her head and cross her arms over her chest, a sign that we had finished for the day and that she could go, at which point I washed my hands, put on my shoes, took my coat, and set out for one of the two restaurants where I always had my lunch, and that after lunch, if I didn't have any business to attend to, or didn't go for a ride on a bus, I would slip into a light slumber; these late afternoon moments were my favourite moments of the day, at least those in which I roamed about my flat (like Benz on the prowl, as Ema says), going out onto the balcony to smoke or gaze into the distance, till evening, when I was beset by dark forebodings . . . so, when I began to realize the orderliness of my days, I also realized that this was all because of Ema.

It was Ema, that raven-eyed, raven-haired woman from Portugal who unlocked my front door every morning at seven-thirty, went into the kitchen, opened the windows, and noisily began preparing my breakfast. It was Ema, with her Lusitanian common sense who had persuaded me over a period of eighteen years that I had to start working at the break of day and not whenever the mood seized me, as I had always done. It was this village woman from Huetor Tahar, where at three in the afternoon you didn't even see a cat on the street, who had introduced me to the virtues of the siesta. It was Ema who had filled my flat with plants that had to be lived with and watered regularly and persistently. She had accustomed me to afternoon tranquillity. To my first cup of coffee, my second, my cold supper in the fridge and the fresh roses on the piano. She had rearranged my books (so that Faulkner stood next to Laclos, and *Lady Chatterley* next to *The Princess of Cleves*), and told my acquaintances and anyone else that I was not to be called whenever they liked, but only between seven and eight in the evening. She had even tamed Benz the untameable, so that he no longer went on the prowl in the afternoons, but only in the evenings. It was Ema Angeles, and no one else.

My daily existence can be divided into two periods: the pre-Ema era, in which I ate when I was hungry, worked when I felt like working, and slept when I could no longer stay awake – an era in which my flat was open to all, as was my bed – and the period after my forty-fifth birthday, the day Baleli suggested I rent out the room on the sixth floor (which was part of my flat, but was of use to no one but the mice) to a young Portuguese woman by the name of Ema Angeles, who in return would see to it that my flat stayed tidy and my shirts impeccable. I remember that I only accepted her suggestion because I was curious to see who the owner of such a promising, rhythmic name might be. When she knocked at my door a few days later – she was a small, stocky woman with black hair, and eyes so dark that the pupils could not be distinguished from the iris – when that same afternoon she rolled up her sleeves and began silently rummaging about my flat, I had no idea how deeply she was to intervene in my ways, nor how unwaveringly she would watch over my flat and my shirts.

Ema is one of those rare women I know whom I have never called anything but Ema and with whom nothing has ever happened, except for a failed kiss in the kitchen a month or so after her arrival, and an embrace in which I threw myself at her feet, an action I now remember as either brotherly or desperate. Needless to say, "nothing" cannot describe eighteen years of what one might call living together. The deep and eloquent silences between us. Ema is not only the woman who brought order to my life, she also taught me how to be silent without feeling uneasy, she taught me how to be silent, as the silence between us was more eloquent than words. Ema and I could say practically anything we had to say to one another without uttering a single word. It was at such moments that she confided in me that although she only touched my books in order to dust them, she knew me better than anyone else. That she knew me because every morning when she put my breakfast on the table and sat down across from me, she would look into my eyes. Because she could read in them and in my face and the agitation of my hands what kind of a night I had spent. Because she could see how time was descending irredeemably upon me. How in these eighteen years my hair had thinned, my shoulders had slumped, my cheeks had sagged, if I may . . . no, please, feel free . . . and I in turn replied that in all those years I had grown accustomed to her hard, ebony eyes and hair, her shuffling steps, our staring at each other every morning. Her secrets, too, and that she never let me cross the threshold of her being. And the order she cast around us like a web, every object in its place, and my day, which she divided as if time had to be divided and poured afresh into little jars, day after day.

When, two days after Farkas's party, I set out for my lunch with the blonde I had accompanied in the taxi, I thought of Ema. And of time which had to be poured afresh into little jars day after day, and of all the things around me that I found every morning in the same place I had left them the night before. The old armchair Baleli gave me, for instance, with its pale yellow lilies, always stands between the fireplace and the bookshelf, always the same distance from the window, and from it every afternoon I gaze at the same piece of sky. As I walked down the stairs I remembered almost with relief that I had not given the blonde the address of the restaurant.

6

If I could write screenplays – I know I am becoming obsessive – I would begin with the restaurant on the boulevard Saint-Germain, with its low chandelier in the middle of the room in the shape of a luxuriant dish from which hang heavy glass grapes intertwined with vine leaves. With its revolving doors, which release client after client into the restaurant in waves. And the young woman among them, who from the first instant attracts our attention. Because of the flowery dress beneath the short velvet coat adorned with a row of sparkling buttons, and the red patent leather handbag in the shape of a heart, which she is holding in front of her with both hands as if it were a chalice. Because of the impression she makes appearing suddenly out of nowhere in this subdued, discreet place with its low lights and voices, even though she is looking around coolly and methodically. She makes her way through the tables with firm steps – a few heads turn – and walks towards the back room which opens out at the rear of the restaurant. She stops beneath the arch of the entrance to the back room. She leans for an instant on the wooden panelling as if to say: Here I am. She takes off her coat, folds it over the arm on which she has her heart-shaped bag – which, as is only now apparent – is the same triumphant red as the tulips on her dress, and walks over to a table. The back room is reserved for regular customers, who clearly feel at home in the *fin-de-siècle* atmosphere of the furniture and the light fittings shaped like hanging grapes. The young woman in the tight dress festooned with tulips, her coat draped over her arm, stops in front of one of the tables at which an elderly man is sitting.

"Hello," she says, almost at the same instant the man turns to her.

"Kati," he mumbles, grave, taken aback – it is obvious that he was not expecting her – and folds the newspaper lying open on the table. He gets up, approaches her, takes her velvet coat, and glances at her red, heart-shaped bag.

"Grushenka," she corrects him.

He gazes at her as if he were trying to remember something. He hands her coat to a passing waiter and whispers a few words to him. The waiter, an eager young man with a sickly complexion, nods and walks away with the coat over his arm. In the archway between the rooms he stops and turns to look back at them: from a distance the two look like strangers on a railway platform who have just got off the same train. The elderly man looks at the young woman as if he were really seeing her for the first time. His eyes light up. She rests her cheek on her palm. The two are leaning towards one another, bathed in the yellowish-orange light of the heavy grapes. Later, during the main course, they are still immersed in conversation, eating, talking, here and there the young woman laughs, the elderly man looks at her, looks at her as if he wants to capture her laugh, her words, the movement of her hands, and the unruly hair that keeps falling across her forehead. Through the filter of coloured light one barely notices that the man is a great deal older than she is. Later again, after the main course, after the table has been cleared, when the man orders a bottle of white Burgundy, fills their glasses, and in a low voice utters a drawn-out phrase, they fall silent. The young woman turns pale, at least from a distance it looks as if she has, toys with a piece of paper . . . picks it up . . . leans over the glass of white Burgundy . . . and later still, when the back room has been empty for some time, they finally get up. The elderly man lays his hand on her shoulder as if they have come to an agreement. Then he looks around the room, suddenly he is in a hurry, he is looking for the eager young waiter, who returns with her velvet coat over his arm. When they walk through the main dining room, now also practically empty, and as they pass beneath the heavy chandelier shaped like a dish with its ebullient grapes and out through the revolving doors, a few curious heads turn, as a person on the street might turn to look at a couple who for some reason or other has caught his attention.

7

"R. A. . . . Tibor," Baleli breathed into the phone in her palest voice later that day. My name, pronounced with that icy pause after its two initials, particularly with the last syllable prolonged, is the way in which my former wife expresses her disappointment in me. The scorn with which she lands on the "R", rasping with the hoarse voice of an old smoker, and the irony which she hangs on the "A", pronouncing it as though she had dropped an armful of porcelain. I have never understood what it was that bothered her about the name, with which I have been signing my books from the very beginning, nor how it managed to become such a harsh pejorative on her lips. Especially since she calls me Tibor, as everyone else around me does. And Tibor, after all, was one of the names of love between us, and later of the kind of attachment that evolves after a marriage that does not last long enough for hatred to begin. It is true that I had refused to tell her what was hidden behind the letters "R" and "A" (I assured her that they did not stand for names but for verbs), even though she persisted, as if these miserable letters had set up an invisible wall between us. But it is also true that Baleli detested the flippancy with which I had invented my name, and the playfulness or mania with which I had transformed her from Élisabeth into Baleli, a name she had grown used to over the years, at times even introducing herself as Baleli Béranger, perpetuating the very thing that was indomitable and inexplicable in me. Then one fine morning she began calling me R.A. . . . Tibor. "Oh, Baleli, Baleli," I had protested, and had sung the first couplet of an old Hungarian ballad. This afternoon too I wanted to say "Oh, Baleli, Baleli," and sing the opening lines of that ballad to her.

I slowly repeated that I had met a young woman whom I intended to marry, and that she, Baleli, was the first person I was telling this. And then I added, in an even lower voice, that I had never thought that anything like this could happen to me.

Suddenly I could hear her breathing at the other end of the line, distinctly, as if she had just surfaced for a few gulps of air. She is going to say something, I thought to myself, anything, R. A. . . . Tibor with that heavy block of ice between the initials and my name.

I could assure her that I was aware that there was something inappropriate in what I was doing, truly inappropriate, particularly since all these years I had been pontificating against marriage as the most effective mechanism for the destruction of love, against the inexplicable urge that drove people to place their heads freely in a yoke, which not even a beast of burden would do – and to do it in triumph and with laurels. We must not forget that I have always been a devotee of secret marriage, as with my Jacob and Agathe, secret and for a prearranged period of time or, as Jacob said at the ceremony, "for as long as the fire for one another burns in our loins". And I am not talking about my claim that I could survive outside any kind of collective life, whether family, army, or religion, a claim I was proud of, especially in view of the list of animals I recited to her the day we dissolved our brief union – leopards, martens, squirrels, badgers, and . . . me. All this is true enough, and it is also true that I have never been a man of principle, even if perhaps I give that impression. What I am trying to say is that I understand that my announcement astonished her. It astonished me too when I suggested it to the young woman sitting opposite me. And perhaps you are right, Baleli. I remember on one of our first mornings, when we woke up together in your bedroom that resembled a junkshop filled with furniture, old porcelain and other curios, and, radiant, you whispered to me that I was your destiny. And I shivered as if I was cold, or as if clouds of dust and spider webs were raining down on me from your abandoned armoires. I felt cornered in the role of your destiny. I did not want to be anyone's destiny except my own, and from that morning on I discarded the word "destiny" in favour of the verb "to want". And "to abandon". To know how to abandon, to turn one's back on, to disappoint, betray . . . But perhaps you are right, Baleli. Not believing in destiny is proof of . . .

She hung up before I had a chance to say more. I stood for a moment with the receiver in my hand. My cat Benz was prowling persistently around my feet. I hung up, picked him up, and sat down in the armchair. He made himself comfortable on my knees and immediately dozed off. The last thing I had wanted to do, I said to myself, was to chatter on about Agathe and Jacob, or about that morning in Baleli's room, and least of all about destiny. I wanted to tell her of my marriage and of something else that was winding its way obstinately and warily through my head, leaving me with a sensation of cold.

For Kati and I had struck a contract. Somewhat like the prenuptial agreement that Baleli and I had made at her family's insistence before we married, specifying that our property was to remain separate. Except that with Kati the agreement was of a very different kind, for which it was not necessary to go to a lawyer or to sign any documents, its main and in fact its only provision having nothing to do with property. It had to do with Kati and me, with our past, our present, and also our future.

After the paper sailboat had become soaked with white Burgundy, Kati sat up, folded her arms, and said, "But we won't ask each other any questions."

Which in other words meant that we would set out as strangers on our road together, and that in a sense we would remain strangers. But strangers who love one another, I whispered. When we got up from the table I rested my hands on her shoulders, and for the first time felt the reckless tenderness of her skin. Strangers who love one another . . . Strangers who love one another . . . If Benz had woken up and been able to form his mouth into a smile, he would have smiled at me condescendingly, just as the tramp had done in the light of the Venetian lamps.

8

Am I a careful man, one who measures every step he takes? Or am I quite the opposite, an adventurer who lets wild currents carry him into the unknown? Do I consider myself one of those men who know how to get what they want? Is man as great as his dreams? And love? Is it not always a new journey towards a destination not of our choosing, and . . .

"Could you repeat that please?" I asked, clearing my throat, taken aback by the last question. In the low-ceilinged radio station the sun flared for an instant like a floodlight. It flashed into my eyes, and I looked down at the floor.

"Before we continue our conversation with today's guest, writer R. A. Tibor, we will hear Amalia Rodriguez, who, he tells me, is one of his favourite singers," the sultry voice of the hostess of the weekly radio show *As You Like It* intoned, with professional self-confidence.

I looked at her in astonishment. She was a young woman with short, platinum-blonde hair and a long neck, and earrings that hung down almost to her shoulders and jangled against her face at the slightest movement. She lit a cigarette and smiled at me through the smoke.

"Amalia Rodriguez?" I asked with a hint of a Portuguese accent.

She drew in another mouthful of smoke and peered at her notes, as if she hadn't heard me. The programme, which was moving into its final section, was evidently going according to plan. She was clearly pleased with herself, pleasantly surprised that she had managed to handle so well a guest like me, known as I am for my unpredictability and arrogance. Amalia Rodriguez was singing: "*Se eu casasse com a filha da minha lavadeira, talvez fosse feliz . . .*" I had the urge to unsettle this self-satisfied hostess just a little, by protesting that I had never mentioned Amalia Rodriguez to her, although I definitely knew the singer better than she did on account of a certain

Portuguese woman by the name of Ema Angeles, who sang Amalia Rodriguez's songs every morning. And that in future I would like the hostess to run her music selections by me, especially if she intended to present them as mine.

She was still leaning over her notes, and I was waiting patiently for her to deign to look up at me, when my eyes happened to rest on her breasts, their roundness rising from the décolleté of her thin blouse. I immediately forgot my intention of settling the matter of Amalia Rodriguez, as my mind wandered to other breasts, those unknown breasts that were soon to live near me, lying beneath the red tulips and the other flowers, silently rising and falling . . . leaning over me at night . . . baring themselves . . . filling my hands . . . and in my thoughts of those future breasts, quite as unknown as the breasts of the talk-show hostess sitting before me, I was overcome for a few moments by a feeling of happiness. Even today, a few long months after that April afternoon in the studio, I remember the pulsation inside me, like the promise of a new season to come. My eyes smarted, although the sun wasn't shining into them as it had been a few moments before. Amalia Rodriguez moaned a few more times "*alma minha, alma minha*," and then fell silent.

The young hostess with the platinum hair finally looked up at me, her earrings, again in motion, jingling lightly against her face as she smiled with a professional air, and in a clear voice repeated her question: "Is not love in fact a journey towards a destination not of our choosing, which turns out to be what we commonly call . . . hell?" And it was the first time since I began participating in this whole charade, which Farkas calls the "campaign against oblivion", that I did not know what to say. A tortured silence ensued. I had not recognized the phrase that I myself had written in one of my first books.

9

Needless to say, I was reckless. I was definitely reckless, marrying a young woman I had just met, of whom I knew only that she was twenty-seven, that she had been born in Italy, in Trieste (according to her passport, which was nonetheless French), that her official name was Grushenka Karst and that she was unemployed. I also knew some of her dresses, particularly the one adorned with red tulips, which I knew best of all, and what she wore beneath them. One could equally say that I had been imprudent to introduce her to Simon Osterman and to ask him to be witness at my marriage.

Simon Osterman is the only man – and I will say this only once – whom I have ever both admired and envied. I cannot say that I admired him for his appearance, though Simon is definitely what one would call a handsome man: tall, with a powerful torso, slicked-back black hair like Ema's, a high, intelligent forehead, and lips that are curved, almost feminine, always ready to break into a beguiling smile or a disparaging sneer. A bout of polio when he was a child left Simon Osterman with a slight limp, but this in no way weakened his standing as a handsome man. Quite the contrary. One had the impression that his slight physical flaw made him even more attractive, and to an extent unreachable. One thing I did not admire or envy was his obvious and astonishing success with women. After the last note died away he would stand on his conductor's podium, shining and spent, like a bird after a long flight over the ocean, and when he turned towards the auditorium the audience, particularly the women, suddenly held their breath. I always felt that they were ready to throw themselves at his feet and remain there for ever. Even though Simon Osterman brought them nothing but sorrow, tears, and even death. His first wife had committed suicide a few years into their marriage. She had left a letter under his pillow, which had slipped under the mattress, so that he did not find it until a few months after her death. In it she wrote, "I shall never ever forgive you for not loving me as much as I loved you. I do not want to live because I do not want to forgive you." He didn't marry the next woman. I met her, she was an Italian by the name of Bianca, and I remember her always with a smile on her face. One night she took Simon's car and went driving down the Paris–Marseilles *autoroute*, ramming at 180 kilometres an hour a Belgian lorry carrying livestock.

It was for something else that I admired and envied Simon Osterman: the impression he gave when he was conducting. For it was as though he was not bound like the rest of us by the laws of gravity. Every time I sat in the auditorium watching his dark, flapping silhouette, I could see with my own eyes that Simon was elsewhere. That on the wings of the music he was able to draw from the orchestra, he soared like a lone bird above the narrow, meaningless, mortal world below. When at the end of a concert Simon turned to face the auditorium, and Simon had a special way of turning to face his audience, one could still detect in him traces of his lone flight. He did not bow, but stood rigid and tall, as if torn from his state of grace and jostled into the narrow world, into this dark auditorium, into an enormous hole that was alien to him, completely alien to him in every way, a hole that wanted to suck him in.

On April 27, 1995, on the threshold of sixty, having lost the last vestiges of reason, I introduced Kati to Simon Osterman a few minutes before we signed our marriage papers at the local registry in the part of town where I used to live. As always, Simon came at the last moment. When he saw us from a distance – Kati's witness was a tall, German girl named Ute, whom I met for the first and last time that day, and Kati was wearing her velvet coat with the sparkling buttons and carrying her heart-shaped handbag – he slowed his pace. When he walks slowly, you can barely notice his slight limp. Also, he wanted to study us at leisure. At first he eyed the long-legged German girl, who was holding a white flower in her hands, in pre-Raphaelite fashion. He obviously mistook her for Kati. Then he eyed me, and I had the impression that beneath his usual friendly and affable expression was an equivocal smile. When he came up to us and I introduced him first to Kati instead of Ute – Kati correcting me, saying that she was not Kati, but Grushenka – he stared at me half-questioning, half-surprised. But he shook hands with Kati as if they were standing on an unfamiliar stage where they would continue to meet, but on which they would never sing a duet, nor have any other scene in common. And then later, after we had signed what we had to sign, and I for the first time really held Kati-Katarina-Grushenka close to me, I noticed with relief that they still were like actors who, though appearing in the same film, did not know one another. Kati was quiet, soft, and tender as a velvet butterfly that by some miracle had alighted near me. Simon moved like an injured bird. And I was anxiously happy.

10

Anxiously happy . . . Marie-Hélène's hands would have frozen for an instant over her keyboard. Anxious, within this nascent happiness . . . No, anxiously happy, I would have repeated, and after a moment's pause Marie-Hélène would have continued typing. She had a deep intuition for word combinations. Not for literature or composition, nor for plots, or characters who she followed with closed eyes. It was an intuition for words more than anything else – for adjectives and metaphors. When the two elements of a metaphor seemed too distant from one another, or too close – hence trite – she raised her hands for an instant, intertwined her fingers or rubbed her palms, one way or another giving me enough time to reconsider.

But for the first time in a long while I am sitting alone in front of my screen, eleven years to be exact, during which time I had become so used to dictating to Marie-Hélène that I sometimes did not even notice her, or I should say that I noticed her only when she left. And yet I studied her constantly, the long, ash-coloured braids that hung over her breasts and the chiselled ears that reminded me of ear-like seashells, so that I often felt that the phrases I uttered and that Marie-Hélène wrote down sprang from somewhere near those shells and from the ash-coloured braids hanging over her breasts, and that I was only deciphering and repeating them. And when I no longer knew how to continue I would eye her silent seashells even more carefully, and listen for their whisper more intently. Or I would get up and begin to pace back and forth in the study. Or I would stop in front of the window and look out at a thick, arc-shaped cloud. Then I would continue my dictation with: "a thick, arc-shaped cloud". With time Marie-Hélène had got used to this. She had got used to the idea that writing might not be as serious a matter as she had thought, and that I might well use anything that came to hand. Her braids, for example, and the reddish blotches around her nose – at least one of my heroines had braids and blotches around her nose – the Spanish hauteur of her head, her brother Paul, who owns a tailor shop and has an apprentice, still almost a boy, whom he ties to the wide cutting table with a string of thread, and the sun expiring before our eyes on the parquet floor, a melon cut in half like bliss to be shared by two . . . and so on and so forth.

Marie-Hélène has not come for some time now. Ema has left. And my cat Benz, who has never failed to return from his prowls, has not come back since yesterday. The one thing that is near me and in my heart these last few days is Katarina-Kati-Grushenka.

II

Paris was our town. Not only because life had placed us both there and because we met there and live there. But mainly because our tale, such as it was and is, could have taken place only in Paris. Nowhere else in the world could our story have been so unforeseeable, so unimpeded, and so merciless, and nowhere else could it have unfolded beneath such an intense sky. Kati seemed to be of the same opinion. We sat drinking champagne with Simon Osterman and Ute on the terrace of one of the cafés near the street I used to live on, Ute caressing her white flower, Kati watching the passers-by, and I wishing I were alone with her. Simon asked nonchalantly when we would be leaving for our honeymoon, and Kati, getting up suddenly, announced, "Right now!"

And when Simon, as taken aback as I was, asked her where we intended to go, she looked at me and said emphatically, "Paris!"

I nodded as if everything had been prearranged. Kati bent forward to Ute and whispered something to her in German, and Ute assumed a grave air and handed her the flower. Then Kati turned to Simon and shook his hand. He looked at her for an instant – evidently he had not expected such an abrupt end to the afternoon – got up, brought his face close to hers, and in an unfamiliar voice mumbled, "I wish you happiness."

Kati nodded pensively and took me by the arm. There was a camera flash from somewhere. We made our way between the tables, carrying the white flower, and again waved goodbye to Simon and Ute from a distance.

When we had disappeared around the first corner and were walking down the rue Saint Benoît, Kati burst out laughing, and held my arm tighter. Clearly she was pleased with herself, and expected me to ask why we had left so hastily. I did not want to disappoint her, but that afternoon I had no need for reasons or explanations. Her laughter and the grip of her hand were all I wanted. And I was more than ready to go anywhere with her. From time to time I even closed my eyes and let myself be guided by her.

Kati was talkative like never before. I listened to her quicksilver voice rushing to talk of Paris, of streets I had never heard of, cemeteries and walkways, hidden passages.

"Hidden passages?" I asked her in astonishment.

"The Passage du Grand Cerf and its merchants of poison . . . The Passage des Princes, which was haunted until not long ago . . . the Passage des Panoramas, where Zola met his Nana . . . the Passage du Prado and its woman with the weasel breasts . . . the Passage Jouffroy . . . the Passage Feydeau . . . Paris must be explored like the body of a lover," she added in a lower voice, and I felt a sharp twinge.

We walked to the Seine and stopped on the Pont Neuf. I thought that she might reveal to me God knows what secret about this old Parisian bridge with its eternally youthful name, or about the two islands in the middle of the Seine, or perhaps about the river beneath us.

"Let us say goodbye to it here," she said, bending over the stone parapet and without ceremony dropping the white flower into the river. I too bent over the parapet and watched the white spot bobbing away.

"Well, that's that," she said after a few moments. I nodded, thinking that life with her would not flow like the Seine beneath us but bubble with joy.

We walked along the northern bank, which she seemed to know better than I did. She took me along narrow streets, past steep façades against which our footsteps echoed. Past Arabian butchers, past stores with brightly coloured gold and silver bales of cloth, mint sellers who laid out their aromatic plants in small pale-green piles, and shadowy bars reeking of alcohol and sweat. We stopped in one and drank a glass of thick, bitter liquid. Kati's face became flushed. She unbuttoned her velvet coat and leaned against me for a moment. The men around us devoured her with their eyes. Tired and starving, we went to a Jewish restaurant near the Parc des Buttes-Chaumont and ordered *caviar d'aubergine* and long thin sausages. We dipped the sausages in a spicy, brownish sauce that burned my mouth and made my eyes water. Kati laughed and poured me some wine. She tore a small piece from the table's paper cover and folded it into a little frog – a toad, she said – and put it next to the spicy sauce to guard me. I gazed at her austere, ivory hands again, her slim fingers with their gracious, round nails, fingers that moved with a mixture of determination and tenderness, giving an impression of autonomy, as if they were marionettes linked to her body and her soul by invisible strings. I caught a finger in mid air and pressed it to my lips. Laughing, Kati pulled it away and ordered two slices of poppy strudel. I was full, and wanted to go to bed with her and forget everything. Everything except her. Who I would soon hold tight on top of me. Who I would hold tight next to me. And then forget her too. Everything. To turn out the light and finally have peace. Kati bit into the poppy strudel and held a piece out to me. I shook my head and said I was going to find us a taxi.

"No, no," she whispered.

I paid, we got up from the table, and she took me by the arm.

Outside, it had been dark for some time. I have always been touched somehow by the stars and by the remnant crescent moon that Farkas made such fun of me over. According to him, my books were teeming with crescent moons. For me the crescent moon symbolized a mysterious continuation, a passage from one phase to another, caterpillar, chrysalis, butterfly . . . Kati and I left the Jewish restaurant arm in arm and crossed to the Parc des Buttes-Chaumont, shivering with cold, Kati buttoning up the gold buttons of her velvet coat as we walked alongside the park. Above us the silvery sickle of the moon shimmered as if it had been painted in a single thin stroke. Kati had fallen silent. She looked around as if we were almost there. The boulevard was nearly empty. I wanted to ask her where we were going, but I didn't. After all, as I have already written, I would have gone anywhere with her. Little by little I no longer felt tired, nor did I feel the cold or the pain in my calves. We had left the park far behind us, crossed a square with two rows of chestnut trees, and were walking along one of the sloping streets when she stopped, sighed, and said, "Here we are."

First I turned to her – her voice had been strangely distant – and then to a narrow building, very low for Paris, that looked as if it had been built in the early twentieth century. Above an arched doorway was the carved figure of a reclining woman with bare breasts, drapery flowing over her hips and thighs. Above her was a red neon sign saying "Hôtel Mon Rêve". Kati walked to the heavy door and pushed it open. Behind it sat an Indian or Pakistani, as if in a pulpit. Kati waited for me to catch up with her, and then said in the same, distant voice of a few moments earlier, "Rooms sixteen and nineteen, please. The name is Tibor."

The Indian or Pakistani got up as if he had been expecting us, picked up some heavy keys, and nodded to us to follow him. We walked along the narrow, badly lit corridor. He unlocked room number sixteen, switched on a red lamp, and turned to us. Kati's face looked distant and astonishingly soft in the reddish-orange light. She touched my neck for an instant, I felt her cold palm, and then she went into her room and shut the door behind her.

12

The following morning I studied myself in my mirror. An old mirror with blackened edges and a gilt frame that Baleli had brought me from Normandy God knows how many years ago, and in which I encounter my face every morning. Baleli had returned from a Sunday trip to the seaside, put the mirror down in front of me and, catching her breath, told me she had bought it as a present for me at a village fair. When I looked into it for the first time, I was a middle-aged man with slicked-back, chestnut hair, a high, ambitious forehead, eyes too close-set and still very blue, and a slightly haughty expression about the mouth – a middle-aged man standing face to face with his former wife with her swanlike neck and the heavy braid of light-red hair hanging over her breast. Then I only saw her heavy braid and her milky neck, and then only her breasts that moved beneath the décolleté of her blouse. That sultry evening, Baleli and I held one another for the last time in front of the new mirror. Baleli arched backward like a strung bow, and wordless and intent I plunged my way into her, and stayed in her, panting, until she let out a muffled cry and became soft as warm wax in my arms. From that day on, from that Sunday evening of our double-portrait in the dusty mirror, my face had imperceptibly, day after day, transformed itself into today's or, to be more precise, yesterday's face.

For when I stepped before the mirror that morning – at

dawn, alone and crushed, I had left the Hôtel Mon Rêve after a sleepless night – I noticed that something had changed. In a single night my face had taken a new direction. I gazed at it for a long time, trying to discern what it might be that had changed so drastically. I knew every detail that one can possibly detect in these morning exchanges of looks with oneself. A new wrinkle by the eye or the mouth that had not been there the night before. A spot or another sign of ageing on the cheeks, the forehead, the temples. The mouth growing thinner, its corners drooping unstoppably downwards. The eyes becoming paler and covered with a yellowish film. Day by day, the folds of extra skin on the neck.

But the new change I saw had nothing to do with this gradual downward progression. I felt that it was of a different kind. I sensed that it was connected to that cruel night in the Hôtel Mon Rêve. To the discovery of how easy it is for the night to be colourless, without substance, and with the cruelty of an x-ray. To my arms that had lain useless on the bed. To my thirsting lips that had wanted to know the taste of her interior. To my slashing thoughts as I strove to understand what was happening. To my pride, my male pride, which I had no idea how to control. To my hope that all this might be just a joke, a prank, a fancy, or perhaps a test which any moment now would come to an end – any moment now she would knock on the door, warm her hands between her thighs, and lie down on me. To my walk through the city in the morning. And to the new day, which for better or for worse had to begin.

13

Kati moved into my flat that same day. When the bell rang and Ema opened the door, Kati was leaning against the wooden panelling, out of breath. An umbrella, a plastic bag, and her red, heart-shaped handbag hung one next to the other on her arm, and in her hand she held some sort of spindly, rootless plant. A large leather bag lay at her feet. Ema looked her up and down. Kati stiffened, and stared back in silence. Their first meeting did not bode at all well. When I appeared behind Ema, Kati looked at me with relief. Her face was clear and rested, and she was wearing her hair up. She held the plant out to me.

"We have to put it somewhere sunny," she said with a serious air, as if nothing at all were the matter. "Not too dry, and not too damp. And there mustn't be a draft. It is very sensitive, because it has to live without earth and doesn't have any roots," she added calmly.

Benz appeared out of nowhere and rubbed against her legs. Ema continued staring at Kati as if she were an apparition.

I introduced her, "Katarina, Kati."

Ema nodded, as she always nodded whenever I introduced her to one of my women, and without saying a word went back to the kitchen. I picked up Kati's bag and closed the door.

She looked around. She walked through the hall, glancing at the photographs on the walls, the carpet, and the old tiled oven, on which she put her umbrella and her plastic bag. She opened the glass-panelled door and went into the blue room with the fireplace, which for the past few years had been my study. She sat down on the yellow armchair, the plant still in her hands. She crossed her legs and looked around, though there wasn't much to see: except for the armchair with its lily pattern, the room was the most austere in the whole flat. Then she went into the adjacent room, which, though the piano took up half the space, served as a sort of reception or living room. The moment she saw the piano, her eyes lit up.

"You play the piano?" she gasped.

I nodded.

"And what about you?" I asked.

"No, I don't," she murmured, picking up one by one the porcelain vases Baleli had given me. She ran her fingers over the sofa that had been pushed up against the piano, and stopped in front of the paintings on the wall. I wanted to tell her about them, particularly the ones by Szinjyei Merse Pal, which were the only ones I really cared for. But Kati was already on the other side of the room, opening the glass-panelled door, and going out onto the balcony.

The balcony was the main artery that led from one side of the flat to the other. One of the reasons why I had settled in this part of town was because of this balcony, with its view over the roofs of Paris and the broad avenues stretching like rivers from the Étoile to the Tuileries, and also because of the name of the street, which at different times I have called Lily of the Valley, Uncle Pons Street, Evgeniya Grandetova, and later Scenes-of-a-Marriage Street and Street of Disillusionment, a street to which I escaped of my own free will, even with relief, from those mainstream-fashionable-literary-artistic-streets.

Kati was carried away by the arterial balcony, and disappeared from my field of vision. I suddenly felt a weariness in my legs and a stinging in my temples, and wondered whether this was the result of our long walk, my sleepless night, the taxi in the morning, or the agitation I felt at this young woman, who, despite everything, was settling down in my flat.

I followed her. I imagined she must be looking at my bedroom, which I knew she would like. There was only a bed and an old oak wardrobe in it. And Ema had planted white onions on the balcony and a robust fern, so that a person who sleeps well could look out of bed in the morning and conjure up the image of breakfast on a lawn. But the bedroom was empty. The bathroom next to it was also untouched.

She had to be in the semicircular room with the cupola, in the far right wing of the flat. A room that served no purpose, even though it was fitted with a bed, shelves, a chest of drawers, and even a washstand. Marie-Hélène had stayed in this room for a few weeks while she had been looking for a flat, but since then the room had remained empty and unused. I stopped at the door. It stood ajar. I pushed it open and entered.

Kati was standing in the middle of the room beneath the cupola. She had unfastened her hair. Her cheeks were red and she was breathing heavily. The plant stood on the chest of drawers near the glass-panelled door. When she saw me, she turned around, waved her arms in the air, and let herself fall back onto the bed. Her breasts rose and fell beneath her tight t-shirt, her legs lay slightly apart.

"This will be my room," she whispered breathlessly.

14

"Cruelty, in literature at least, is a sign of being chosen," I read on a folded piece of paper, which turned out to be a prescription. I have never systematically written down the thoughts of philosophers or my literary peers. When I come across a phrase, an idea, or a word that has somehow caught my attention, I jot it down on the first piece of paper to hand. But many of these papers have fallen victim to my non-archival nature, Ema's sense of order, and her limited regard for ideas. When, like this morning for instance, I open a novel by Balzac (as I live on a street that bears his name, I like occasionally to browse through his novels), and find among the first pages a folded piece of paper on which I had written that phrase about cruelty, I have the impression that it is doubly important: first, because it had concerned me at the time I jotted it down, and second, because it had turned up at this moment, quite by chance, today of all days. With age I have become sensitive to signs, or rather to a certain kind of fatalism. I tend to try and find a deeper meaning to everything, though I am quite aware that the meaning is not always particularly deep.

"The more gifted the writer, the more he will tend to place his characters in dead-end situations. He pursues them, tyrannizes them . . ." (here the words became almost illegible) ". . . forces them to confront every aspect of the impasse they are in, and their . . ." (for a long time I did not manage to make out the last word) ". . . agony", was written in pale letters on the back of the prescription. I turned the paper over – it was a prescription for Morphylon, my old sleeping pills. This prescription in aid of good literature was dated September 17, 1974 – almost twenty years ago. Twenty years ago I needed sleeping pills and sound advice in order to become one of literature's chosen few.

I approached Kati as she lay on the wrought-iron bed, her legs still apart. I gazed at the milky, almost transparent skin of her thighs. I took a step forward. My vision blurred. Kati was staring up at the cupola. I knelt beside her. I laid my head on her stomach, which sank softly beneath my weight. I reached my hand towards the silken area between her thighs . . . Suddenly the x-ray night at the Hôtel Mon Rêve disappeared . . . the morning taxi ride . . . the empty bedroom . . . all that remained was this semicircular room with the cupola that began to pulsate, and the milky whiteness between her legs. Until I felt her cold palm on my shoulder, brusquely pushing me away.

"Tibor!" she shouted in a rough voice. "This is my room!"

She got up and walked past me towards the round table. Her face had become pale, and blue veins stood out on her temples. I remained lying in front of the narrow iron bed as if I had just been pulled out of water.

Well, I am obviously heading in the right direction, I thought to myself, not without bitterness, as I left Kati's new room by way of the arterial balcony. In the right direction to join the chosen few of literature. My tale will contain a good dose of cruelty, dead-end situations, perhaps even agony . . . only this time I shall not only be the author, but also one of the main characters.

15

I have always been of the opinion that women talk more openly about sex than men. When I say women, I mean not only women writers, even though I have had ample opportunity to confirm that this is true, that it is easier to believe them, that one can learn quite a few things from them about which we, their male colleagues, for all kinds of reasons, remain silent. And particularly that under their pens sex, in other words what we call the relationship between men and women, is more real. I am thinking of women in general. Of Silvia, for instance, a specialist in late Gothic art and a simultaneous interpreter, who was my best sexual partner. In a few afternoons with her I picked up more information about the troubled waters of eroticism than I could have gleaned from the most exhaustive and up-to-date manuals on the subject. Between coffee and cream cake in the old Danubian café across the street from the medical faculty, and the fitting room of an elegant boutique in which she tried on every piece of clothing on sale, Silvia revealed to me in the chattiest and most nonchalant fashion things about my sensual nature I hadn't even dreamed of. When, like today, I think about my sexuality, and when I want to avoid being too indulgent with myself, I try to remember Silvia's words.

When we first slept together – on a windy autumn afternoon when the last leaves were falling on the boulevard Voltaire – she leaned over me and told me that I was a damn Puritan.

"And pretty inhibited too," she added, as we took a shower together in her bathroom.

"Who'd have thought!" she continued, as she spread soap over her inviting body. "R. A. Tibor, with his broad shoulders, his elegant shirts and cufflinks! The way he walks! The controlled movement of his hips! One look at how a man walks, and you know who you are dealing with. It's like at a dance where you can pick a partner with your eyes shut!"

In short, she had been mistaken about me, which did not happen to her all that often, she said, laughing as she vigorously towelled both of us dry.

"But a man's sensuality can easily sprout new shoots and re-blossom, even in full maturity," she said, linking her arm in mine as we walked through the fallen leaves of the boulevard Voltaire.

Later, either because she had amended her diagnosis, or because she had helped bring forth the new shoots that she had predicted beneath the bare trees of the boulevard Voltaire, we began seeing each other regularly: in her attic, in cheap hotels on the outskirts of Paris, in obscure museums and out-of-the-way restaurants, in movie theatres, in deserted parks. For Silvia immensely enjoyed making love in the most impossible places.

"You can't have eroticism without a few drops of perversion," she assured me. "All I need is a little dose of danger . . . the possibility that we might get caught . . . that someone might be peeking at us – an invisible presence – voyeurism at bargain prices. But you are more complicated than that."

"Complicated?" I asked, taken aback by this tiny Frenchwoman of Italian descent, whom I called "my kitty cat", who turned out to be not only the most skilful lover I have ever had, but also the most sharp-eyed.

"Well – what attracts you to women, what whips up your imagination and your senses, is a mix of abandon and reserve," she said, as if this were her final pronouncement.

And it was. Shortly thereafter, Silvia moved to Lyons. She did come back to Paris from time to time, but invariably only for an afternoon, or for an evening party, which barely gave us a few moments for a quick love session. And so our deep conversations about love, our chats in the Viennese café and the fitting rooms of some elegant boutique came to an end.

We saw one another for the last time a few years ago. I wanted to surprise her. I invited her to one of the most discreet and expensive Parisian hotels. But the effect was the exact opposite of what I had intended: as we washed away the damp traces of love in the large bathroom with its ceramic tiles, she whispered that I had tricked her. I thought she was referring to the fading luxury of the hotel room or the anonymity of the ceramic bathroom, and I wrapped her tiny body in the bathrobe provided by the hotel. But after this encounter she never called me again, and I didn't have her number.

If I had her number now, I would dial it immediately and ask my kitty cat the following questions in the name of the unique liaison I had had with her: in what way had I tricked her at the Hôtel Raphaël, how was I complicated, and how should I approach this young woman by the name of Kati-Katarina-Grushenka who is lying asleep not far from me.

16

How should I approach this young woman by the name of Kati-Katarina-Grushenka who is lying asleep not far from me? I suddenly felt hot, as I always do when I wake in the early hours of the morning after a few hours of troubled sleep – usually the end of my night's rest. It was just before dawn, when the rue Balzac lies in its deepest slumber. Darkness gradually receded. The silhouettes of the houses lining the avenue stood like grey dominoes. The eastern sky began to lighten. Any moment now the sun would free itself from behind the roofs. The first drops of light trickled towards me. The sky above remained patiently drab while bright pastel colours began to fill the horizon. To my misfortune I knew these moments of the awakening day by heart, and I am prepared to wager that in this entire Parisian neighbourhood there is no better authority on the dawn than I. I wiped the sweat from my forehead, neck, and shoulders, wrapped myself in my dressing gown, and went out onto the balcony.

It will be a nice day today, I said to myself, and immediately thought of Kati. A week had passed since she had moved in at number 73, Scenes-of-a-Marriage Street. During the day she was cheerful and relaxed. We went shopping. We bought all sorts of things. Kati didn't have Baleli's intuition, or her unerring taste in objects – china, clothes, furniture. And yet it was a delight to go shopping with her. A Turkish rug merchant engaged us in conversation and offered us mint tea. We sat on the floor, Kati taking off her shoes, leaning back against a pile of carpets, and letting her hair tumble on them. Every day we brought new things home. Forks, for instance, cups which we found in the rue du Bac, an Anatolian kilim bought from the Turkish merchant, which Kati managed to haggle down to a third of the price. Ema silently watched the growing clutter, noise, and dust. She bit her lip, her eyes flashed, but she kept out of Kati's way, as if her moving into the flat was merely a temporary arrangement. Towards evening, Kati became irritable and ill-tempered, locked herself in the semicircular room with the cupola, and wanted nothing to do with me.

Yesterday we went for a walk beneath the flowering acacia trees along the avenue Carnot. She picked up some lilac-coloured blossoms and slipped them into my pocket. I caught her hand, closed my eyes, and kissed her open palm.

"What a sweet, sweet hand," I whispered into her palm, nestling it against my face. "Spend the night with me – be mine."

Kati tugged her hand away and moved back a step.

"If you could only see how ridiculous you look, Tibor," she exclaimed.

"Ridiculous?" I repeated, the way I do when I am taken aback, or when I am at a loss for words, though I feel a mute, impotent anger rising within me. She took a pocket mirror out of her handbag and held it up to my face. On top of everything she is adept at making a fool of me, I thought bitterly, and glared brusquely into the mirror. A second later we both burst out laughing. I looked like a clown, my face covered with yellow acacia pollen, as were her hands. Kati came close to me and with her spit wiped the yellow from my face. I felt her breath, and was almost happy again. Then she leaned against me and said that she was going out that evening. "Alone. You needn't wait up for me, Tibor," she added, patting my neck with the palm of her hand.

I waited for her until my eyes began to burn. I kept tossing and turning. Where could she be? With whom? A few days earlier she had told me that she wanted to sign up for some exercise classes.

I tightened the belt of my dressing gown. I went out onto the arterial balcony. I stopped before the glass-panelled door of the semicircular room with the cupola. The door stood ajar; it was covered with a curtain that Kati had made out of old lace. I stood before the curtain for a while and tried to make out her shape in the bed through the holes in the fabric. I felt a chill. Just watch me catch cold on top of everything, I said to myself. Softly I pushed against the panel of the door. I did not want to wake her. In the past few days I had given up trying to find reason in my actions. I only wanted to see her, to make sure that everything was all right.

Everything was all right. Very much all right, if I may say so. At first I saw her head, tilted, half-hanging off the edge of the pillow and the bed. Her shoulder peeked out from under the covers, and her hand was clutching it . . . I imagined her legs drawn up beneath the covers . . . I took another step forward. Behind her head, facing her, lay another head. Dark, with short, coarse hair, an unshaven face, a dark neck, and a hairy chest on which a hand was resting. On its middle finger shone a silver ring with a blue stone. I was surprised again by the oddity of my perception, which at moments of extreme intensity tends to focus on the most trivial and banal details. Like this silver filigree ring with a blue stone on the middle finger of the hairy hand of a man.

I do not know how long I stood gazing at it. As I turned and walked towards the door, my feet got tangled in a piece of clothing lying on the floor, and I almost fell. I had the impression that somebody stirred in the bed behind me. I pushed the curtain back and went out onto the balcony.

17

"Congratulations, you son of a lion!" Farkas shouted in his powerful baritone, slapping me on the back. "Who'd have thought it possible! Who'd have thought it possible? One, two, three, and it's a done deal! And behind our backs, too! A poacher often bags his best doe well after the season. He comes face to face with her on the savannah, lowers his rifle, and picks up the doe, the pretty little doe, in his arms. He hides her from all the world. Doesn't breathe a word about her to anyone. But I knew you were up to something, you son of a lion!"

"Now, Farkas," I tried to interrupt, though I knew quite well that it was impossible to stop him. I was exhausted. My eyes ached. I fought to chase away the image of the closely cropped head in Kati's bed, and its hand with the silver ring. I listened to Farkas absently, though I eyed him intently. He was pacing up and down my study without having taken his jacket off or asked Ema for his usual *café au chocolat*. When Farkas finds a bone, he will gnaw at it to the bitter end. When he falls into a whirlpool, he lets it carry him away.

"Do you remember that afternoon at the Petit Philosophe? We were frozen through, and ordered some grog – out on the terrace while everyone else was holed up inside. Do you remember, you son of a lion, the conclusion we reached about women and literature?"

I tried to remember what conclusion we had reached about women and literature, and pointed at the armchair, hoping that he would finally sit down. His pacing back and forth was making me even more nervous than ever. Farkas is both my publisher and my agent – a good publisher and a good agent, although since I have never had another publisher or agent I cannot really make a comparison. But it is quite possible that without him I would not be the R. A. Tibor I am today, just as Editions F. Farkas would perhaps not be what it is without me. Undoubtedly, Farkas and I met at the right place and the right time. We come from practically the same country, and our fatherlands were the first thing we wanted to rid ourselves of. One's fatherland is one's ball and chain, roots are tantamount to slavery, we declaimed, citing our more or less celebrated statelessness. Both of us, each for his own reasons, wanted to lose himself in the wide world and find himself anew. Farkas was inventive and crafty, I was proud and self-assured. The heavens seemed to smile upon us, even when darkened by heavy clouds.

He didn't want to sit down. Finally he stopped pacing the room and leaned against the fireplace. He looked happy, rested, and his small brown eyes peered at me with curiosity.

"You could at least have dropped me a hint or something, you son of a lion! A little hint, nothing more! But no, Farkas, as always, is left in the dark."

I had no idea what he was talking about. I wanted to get up and have Ema bring him his *café au chocolat*. He took a newspaper out of his bag and slowly began leafing through it in front of me. He stopped at the last page and held it up to my face, pointing to a black and white photograph at the bottom which I easily recognized as myself and Kati, one of her hands clinging to me, the other holding a long white flower. Written in bold letters beneath the picture was: "R. A. Tibor: his bride or an adoring fan?"

"His bride is what I've been telling everyone for the past few days," Farkas said. "I don't know if you're aware of this, Tibor, but you have quite a female following. Take that radio talk-show hostess, for instance. She keeps asking if it's really true that R. A. Tibor has gone and got himself married or if it's all a hoax. No, he's got himself married, is what I tell every one of them. I only hope that these women readers of yours won't desert you now."

I folded the newspaper and handed it back to him. He put it on the mantelpiece and turned again to look at me. Farkas is a tall man with broad shoulders, wide hips, a small head, fleshy lips, and a pencil moustache.

"Where's the doe? Is she still asleep?" he asked after a few moments, finally unbuttoning his jacket.

I nodded and even tried to smile. The doe . . .

"No, I understand, I understand perfectly well," he said in a lower voice.

Finally we fell silent, and finally our eyes met. I wanted to ask him what it was that he understood, I wanted to ask him in all earnestness, without the slightest hint of irony, to ask him as a friend, because I myself in the last few days, particularly in those early morning hours, had done little else but try to understand. After all, Farkas was also my friend, one of my oldest friends, and his intuition is very sharp indeed.

There were light, gliding steps outside in the hall. A moment later the door opened hesitantly. We looked at the slight figure in woollen stockings, white nightdress and pullover, carrying a tray with two cups and a sugar bowl. Kati came over to us almost silently, her eyes fixed on the liquid quivering in the cups. The doe . . . She put the tray on the table and gave a sigh of relief. Then she came up to me, leaned her face towards my ear, and I smelled again the peach aroma of her hair.

"Did you sleep well, Tibor?" she whispered.

I wanted to look her in the eye. But Kati did not move away, as if she perhaps intended to say something more. Then she stood up straight, pulled her hair back behind her ears, and went over to Farkas. She held out her hand.

"Katarina," she said loudly, and then in a softer voice, "Kati."

As she shook hands with Farkas, she glanced at me with a confiding smile.

Farkas held her hand for a long time, repeating over and over, "Pleased to meet you, so very pleased to meet you – and thank you for the coffee."

"*Au chocolat*," Kati said, handing him the cup. "Two spoons of coffee and two spoons of dark cocoa mixed with boiling water."

Suddenly I had a dark premonition.

"Where is Ema?" I asked her.

She picked up the second cup and handed it to me.

"She's left," she murmured.

18

She's left! She's left! I hurried down the hall. I looked in the kitchen . . . in the bedroom, the bathroom, the room with the piano . . . even in the semicircular room with the cupola. I went up to the sixth floor, knocked on the door to Ema's room. Silence, there was nobody there. Footsteps in the flat next door; voices, a radio.

I sat down in front of her door. I buried my face in my hands. I decided to wait for her. Regardless of how long it took. I wanted to explain everything to her, to make everything clear, to talk to her. To sit on her sofa that sagged lightly beneath my weight.

I had been in her room only once. Ema had never invited me. One evening, however, in a café across from Farkas's place, somebody stole my jacket, which among other things had my keys in it. I wound up standing at my door in my shirtsleeves. Then, like today, I climbed up to the sixth floor, sat down on the last step, and waited. Like today, it was almost spring. Ema came home late at night, her cheeks chafed and her eyes sparkling as if she had just made love. Through her light summer dress I could see the outline of her round hips, her tiny waist, and her ample breasts. I liked looking at her powerful torso. She looked at me with a mixture of surprise and irritation, but she did invite me in. She had me sit on the sagging sofa. She offered me some port and sat down on a chair next to the sofa. Her room was clean and tidy, though crammed with jarringly coloured objects – furry toys on the bed across from the sofa, a stuffed weasel on top of the kitchen cupboard, a piece of cloth with embroidered red-and-yellow carnations hanging on the wall. On the table was an ashtray shaped like a woman's hand. Ema pushed it towards me and said I could smoke if I wanted to.

I wanted to, I told her, and lit a cigarette. I was in no hurry. I poured myself another glass and asked her why she wasn't drinking. She rose and got herself a glass. On the sideboard stood a row of picture frames adorned with shells, containing photographs of an adolescent boy. Thirteen or fourteen years old. Perhaps even older. Wearing glasses, with a self-conscious smile on lips above which light down was beginning to grow. In one of the photographs he was almost a child. No glasses, wearing short trousers, a yellow bird in his hands. I wanted to ask her if this was her son, what his name was, and why she had never told me that she had a son back in Portugal. I remembered that the one condition of her moving in was that I gave her a vacation in the summer and at Christmas. I decided not to ask her any questions. I poured us another glass of port. It was none of my business if she didn't want to tell me anything about the boy. As it was, I barely knew anything about her. I was aware that she knew a guard at the Rothschild Museum, that he often called her, and that he kept chickens and a rooster in the museum's backyard, letting them out into the park in the evenings. Perhaps he was more than just an acquaintance. His name was Manuel. Perhaps she had spent the evening with him. In the narrow building next to the Palais Rothschild. I looked at her. Her cheeks had regained their milky colour, but her eyes continued to sparkle darkly. We looked at one another. We looked at one another as if we were taking each other by the hand. Peacefully, quietly, simply, like two beings who, late at night, are sitting side by side drinking port, smoking, and understanding one another. Without a word, without anything. I remember feeling the heat of her gaze. But my verbal nature nagged at me, I wanted to say something to her, particularly about what I was feeling right then. My special feeling. A good feeling, a very good feeling indeed, almost as if we had just made love and were now smoking a cigarette, soothed, tranquil, and at the same time slightly disconcerted by our incursion into one another. Had she not stood up, I would perhaps have told her all this. But Ema, God knows why, quickly got up and walked over to the sideboard. She took the key to my flat from a hook and placed it in front of me. I eyed it as if it were a rival. But after all I had come here for the key I told myself, and picked it up.

"Good night, Ema."

A tall, thin man came out of the neighbouring flat, locked the door with a heavy bunch of keys, and stalked past me on his giraffe-like legs. At the bottom of the stairs he looked back up at me, half-surprised, half-indifferent. I must look like a walking disaster, I thought. My back began to ache. I'll take a walk over to the Rothschild Museum, I said to myself. Of course, why hadn't I thought of it earlier. Perhaps I'll find Manuel there.

I walked down the rue Balzac. The museum and the park were just a stone's throw away. Since I have lived on this street I have often gone for walks in the park – I've seen Manuel's chickens, for instance – but I have never been to the museum. My footsteps crackled on the fresh gravel. I stopped in front of the narrow house in which the guard lived. I rang once, twice, as instructed by the metal plate. Nobody answered. I rang a third time. Still nobody. I tried to enter the park through the open basement. A woman sitting in the cashier's booth shook her head decisively, and with both hands motioned that there was an entrance to the park on the other side. I walked around the wall. I sat down on the first empty bench beneath an ancient tree and closed my eyes.

I was awakened by the shouts of little children and a slightly older boy, who was tapping me on the knee with his plastic spade.

19

The following day Ema and I said goodbye. As she did every morning, she placed a cup of black coffee in front of me along with a few slices of toast, butter, and one of her homemade jams. But this time she did not put her own cup on the table. She did not sit down next to me and roll down her sleeves as she always had. She busied herself about the kitchen with her back turned. When I had finished my breakfast she cleared away the toast and jam and carefully wiped the table. Only then did she sit down across from me as she did every morning. She sat there motionlessly, her arms folded. Then she slipped her hand into her pocket, and placed her key in front of me, just as she had done that day in her room.

"What happened, Ema?" I asked hastily.

She got up and straightened her skirt.

"Nothing," she answered.

She had evidently prepared herself for our last morning together. I noted that she had put on her Sunday best and that her hair was tied at her nape in a tighter bun than usual.

"I will vacate my room by this evening. I would be grateful if I could leave a few things here till the end of the week."

I got up. I waved my hand nervously in response, even though she was looking down at the floor.

"What do you mean 'nothing'?" I exclaimed.

"I told the young lady about the plants on the balcony and the lime tree in the piano room. That she's got to water it every evening. I've also told her what to do with Benz, and I gave her the address for the coffee shop, the cheese shop on the rue Poncelet, and the drycleaners . . ."

"Ema!" I interrupted her, almost imploringly. "Tell me what happened!"

Only now did she look me in the eye. O her boundlessly speaking eyes, which one enters as one does a long corridor with countless doors. I immediately saw that she would tell me nothing, and that nothing I said would make her change her mind. That she had reached a decision, a final decision. That Kati had something to do with it. That this was probably the last time she and I would see each other. That she would quietly move out of the room on the sixth floor and leave the rue Balzac as quickly and as simply as she had arrived. Ema Angeles, my unswayable, raven-haired, raven-eyed woman from Portugal. I also saw that it wasn't a simple matter for her. That she too had become used to me and to all the trivial everyday things that made up our life together: first coffee, second coffee, watering the plants, vacuuming, shopping, the drycleaners, a cold dinner in the kitchen, flowers on the piano. After all, we had lived side by side for almost eighteen years. After all, we had slipped beneath each other's skin . . . each in our own way, obviously. Ema with her silence and those corridors in her eyes, the doors of which I had learned to open over the years . . . and me . . . me . . . no, today she did not want to talk about me. These past few days she has no longer understood me . . . not that it really mattered to her . . . no, she didn't want to talk about that at all . . . not about me, not about that woman who had moved into the semicircular room with the cupola and who . . . no, she absolutely did not want to talk about her . . . She was going to vacate the room upstairs . . . drop off the key . . . and *Adios señores*.

She looked down at the floor. So that was that.

"Ema," I said, and went towards her. I wanted to tell her how on her account I had waited in the park in front of the Rothschild Museum, that I had fallen asleep, and that a child had hit me in the knee with his plastic spade. But just at that moment Ema turned to the fridge and put the butter away. Ema always knew how to turn her back on my impulses at crucial moments. She looked around the kitchen one last time – everything was in its place – ran her fingers over the counter between the fridge and the sink, and without looking at me again walked out the door. I never saw her up close again.

Kati came back late in the afternoon. From the library, the pharmacy, the paint shop, she shouted from the hall. I heard her taking a shower in the bathroom. Then she opened the door to my study. She came up to me almost on tiptoe, as if she did not want to disturb me, to break the silence of the flat or the silence between us. She sat on my lap and laid her arms around my neck. I felt her freshly bathed skin. She had never before pressed herself so close to me.

"Now we are finally alone," she said, taking my hand in hers.

20

I have written a few novels with love at the centre. Love propelled the action, gave it fresh blood, but wasn't at the heart of things, I thought to myself the following day on a number 31 bus.

The story of Agathe and Jacob, for instance, is a story of love between Agathe – a forty-year-old scientist, a specialist in supernovas, wife of a famous journalist, and mother of fifteen-year-old Louise – and the much younger Jacob, an idle, impetuous, somnambulant man. But the story of Agathe and Jacob is also a story of terrorism and politics, and the hypocrisy of the political world. And also about death. About the death of stars and the death of people. About the boundlessly large and the boundlessly small.

The story of Anna and Lorenzo is also a love story, but at the same time it is very much a novel about appearances, a sort of inverted *Picture of Dorian Grey*. Anna is a sculptress who has been commissioned to make a sculpture of Lorenzo Bosco. She is like a swallow, fluttering and whirling irrepressibly, vehemently, untiringly around Bosco, until she extracts from his massive, ungainly body all the beauty and grace of his soul.

I could also cite Vladimir, Minayev, and Sophie of *Sophie's Serenade*, or Liza P. and Jernejo B. of *Our Last Nights*. And also Peter Holz, with his violent and suffocating love for Peter Holz Jr, his son. But none of these novels deal exclusively with love, none breathe love's oxygen alone, none are imprisoned within love's bare walls.

When a few days after Ema's departure I began writing this

text without a set plan or direction, I had no idea where it would take me. Besides which, it had been quite a while since I had written anything serious, as Farkas had taken to reminding me almost every day. And I was now doing my own typing. Marie-Hélène had fallen ill. When she phoned me after Ema's departure and told me in a timid voice that she was still sick, and didn't know when she would be back, I realized that I would no longer hear her ear-shaped seashells or watch her ash-coloured braid brushing over her breasts. It wouldn't surprise me if Kati also had something to do with this, although she and Marie-Hélène never actually met. Be that as it may, I felt as though the world around Kati and me was closing in on us, or rather diluting itself, and that everything which in the past had formed a kind of ring around me was now widening and opening out. Baleli, Farkas, Picardy . . . even Simon Osterman . . . even the Friends of Rossini Association (the only organization I have ever joined in my life). And for some time now I had no longer been buying newspapers or listening to the news. Somehow the human heart, its miseries, its dark and murky depths, no longer interested or attracted me. I was only interested in and attracted to one heart. A heart I had blindly embraced one afternoon in a restaurant I used to go to. A heart that from that time had been beating almost within my reach.

The text that I began writing a few weeks after Ema's departure and Kati's declaration that the two of us were now alone will be a tale of the beating of our two hearts, and of nothing else.

21

Obviously, I never thought that Ema's departure and Benz's disappearance (Benz, too, disappeared a few days after Ema left) were essential preliminary moves in our life together, Kati's and mine, or, I should say, the grand scene that we had to act out alone, without an audience. Had I realized this, I would not have scoured the neighbourhood from the rue Balzac all the way to the rue du Faubourg Saint-Honoré and the avenue Hoche. I would not have waited patiently for Benz to deign to return from his unexpectedly long jaunt. And I would not have badgered my neighbours, particularly Monsieur Jansen, with a barrage of questions, or begged the concierge not to close her window at night. Benz was in the habit of jumping onto her windowsill so she would open the front door for him. I would have told myself that Benz was an animal I had found at my door one evening, to whom I had offered food, a roof over his head, and later even a kind of benevolence, and who had one fine day decided not to come back to me – Benz is the most indomitable and temperamental cat one can imagine – or I should say decided to abandon me.

And this at the worst point in my life – and yet, who knows, perhaps the best. I was nearing my sixtieth birthday. In a sense I had left two lives behind (of which the Parisian one was more real to me than the other), a few books (of which only two, well, perhaps three, are good through and through), a short-lived marriage to Élisabeth Béranger, a few major and many minor loves (among which I am not including the exquisite liaison with Silvia, my kitty cat), a more or less faithful and arduous friendship with Farkas, another friendship, less intimate and more reserved, with Simon Osterman, one of the greatest conductors of the younger generation, my wordless coexistence with Ema Angeles, and, last but not least, my long relationship with that obstinate, indomitable, black and white cat by the name of Benz. I left behind a few ordeals and crises (which I would prefer not to mention at this point), pretty foreseeable ones at that, and any sense of self-preservation. That day at the restaurant on the boulevard Saint-Germain, when I asked Kati-Katarina-Grushenka to come live with me and to be my wife, I probably committed the single most imprudent and perhaps even self-destructive act of my entire life. I opened myself at the last moment, *in extremis* one might say, to my first true adventure, which only assumed its full dimension after Ema and Benz left me, when Kati and I remained alone on the fifth floor of the house on Scenes-of-a-Marriage Street.

22

I leaned over her sleeping body. Kati's breath, though she was in a deep sleep, was fitful and irregular. Now and then she panted violently, gasped, and then immediately calmed down, as if by an unfathomable caprice of the air in her lungs.

I had never before seen her so close. Never before had her face offered itself to me so generously. Her skin was truly the colour of honey. Sweet, I thought, and shuddered as if my body was about to be seized by convulsions. I could lick her from head to toe. Her loins. Her armpits. Between her knees. The inner side of her arms. Her neck. Behind her ears. Between her legs. Deeply, thirstily between her legs. The sweetest mead. Tasting her meady colour. Entering its sweetness.

Her breath flared up again. She is dreaming, I thought. Those morning dreams that are almost within one's reach. O Kati, I nearly whispered, do not give yourself up to nightmares . . . Turn your back on them. She stirred as if she had heard me, sighed deeply, and clasped her shoulder with her hand. Later I realized that she almost always slept in this position – her arm wound around her shoulder as if she were pinning herself down.

Her face – especially turned as it was towards the window – was a touch lighter than her body. Big as my open palm. In sleep more delicately sculpted. Her chin. Her rippling lips. Her long, straight nose with its delicate nostrils (women with short noses have always struck me as shallow and frivolous). Her high cheekbones. Less perfect was her forehead, of protestant dourness, almost harsh, and there was a longish scar above her right eyebrow, like a sharp slash with a knife, which I had never noticed before. Kati did not like her forehead, and covered it with a casual fringe of blonde hair, just as she did not particularly like her eyes. Mundane, she called them. Vague. But she was proud of her lips, and by extension, of her mouth. The rest of her body, which she submitted to a severe inspection, she felt was not worth mentioning. I have never understood the critical view young women have of their bodies. It is only later in life that they learn to love them when, in a sense, it is already too late. I will teach Kati to love her body now, to be proud of it in time, to offer it up, to relinquish the reins. O sovereign proprietress of mead, I suddenly thought, envisioning a small but tangible mission, the first of many, and perhaps one of the few that might actually prove successful.

And yet at the same time I reflected that things could not have begun on a worse footing. All I had to do was look at the two of us from a distance: a young woman, sleeping almost nude in a wrought-iron bed, and a man with pain-filled eyes wearing pyjamas and a dressing gown, half-kneeling, half-sitting at its foot. Or to think back to our first night at the Hôtel Mon Rêve. The head with the closely cropped hair and the hand with the silver ring on a hairy chest. And I will not even mention the evening two days ago, when Kati, in the middle of dinner at an Italian restaurant on the corner of avenue Lord Byron, between the *spaghetti alle vongole*, the *Chianti classico*, and her theory about pavements (had pavements been wider, our lives would have been significantly different), suddenly looked at her watch, her face growing serious, got up, leaned on my shoulder for an instant, said that she had to meet someone – what a pity, she added – and from a distance, beyond the glass door, waved goodbye to me, the way only she can wave goodbye to me – a hurried wave, as if we barely know each other.

23

Who was the man with the closely cropped hair and the silver ring? How did he end up in her bed? Who had she gone to meet that evening when the two of us were dining at the Italian restaurant on the corner of the avenue Lord Byron? Does she really take exercise classes on Fridays? Who sent her the letter in the light-blue envelope, her name and address written in a shaky hand? Why does she moan in her sleep? What is she up to on those long afternoons, where has she been when she comes into my room at the end of the day, drops her heavy bag, and breathlessly leans over me? Why does she close her eyes when she sits on my lap and has me wrap my arms around her?

The only thing I knew with absolute certainty about her – even if it sounds somewhat ridiculous – was the degree of her long-sightedness: +3.1 in her right eye, and +0.75 in her left.

Late one afternoon, a few days after Benz's disappearance (which Kati did not want to discuss, although she helped me to look for him), Kati and I were in the blue room. The street below was already dark, but we were still bathed in the last rays of the day's sun. Kati was walking up and down the room in shorts, drying her hair with a towel. I was sitting at the table, trying to read at least the first few pages of a manuscript that Farkas had sent to me for an evaluation. The opening lines of a text, as I like to tell Farkas, have to be like an elastic band stretching from the very first sentence to the last, so that you feel the tension throughout. Kati came and stood behind me, leaned over the manuscript, a few drops of water falling onto it, and began to read, "Childhood is like a large bowl of murky water . . . which one fine day must be seized with both hands and . . . poured into the nearest gutter. The question I asked myself that day in early spring . . ."

I turned towards her. Kati raised her head slightly.

"Go on," I said.

"The question I asked myself that day early in spring . . ."

I saw that she was trying to position her head at the right distance from the manuscript, her eyelids fluttering lightly. "... a question I wanted to find the answer to, as if it were a matter of life and death ..."

She abruptly straightened up and, annoyed, continued drying her hair.

"Kati, you have a problem with your eyes!" I exclaimed.

"Yes, sometimes I do," she replied, vehemently continuing to dry her hair.

The following day I made an appointment for her with an optician recommended to me by Farkas's secretary. I thought Kati would protest loudly, or at least snap at me that I should mind my own business, that these were her eyes after all. But she looked at me almost thankfully and murmured, "You will come with me, won't you?"

Towards the end of the week, we took the Métro to a provincial-looking street near the Place d'Italie. "Docteur Guido Plassmann", was written on the door of one of the two-storey buildings overgrown with ivy. I sat down in the waiting room and gazed out at the leaves hanging over the window. I thought of my grandparents' house at the edge of the village, which had been just as overgrown with ivy, and how for years and years I hadn't thought of them, they were at the very bottom of my memory. Kati remained a long time behind the heavy, massive door. The door finally opened, and she stood there looking at me absently. She seemed smaller than usual, and her bare arms protruding from her dark-blue, sleeveless dress struck me as being too long.

"I think it was high time I saw the doctor. +3.1 in my right eye, and +0.75 in my left."

Doctor Plassmann, a middle-aged man with thinning hair and a heavy, ungainly body on which hung a baggy grey suit, came out after her and turned to me.

"+3.1 in the right eye," he echoed, in a voice so low and colourless that I had to lean forward. "A case of juvenile hypermetropia. The eye stopped developing at the age of seven or eight. Needless to say, the problem should have been seen to at the time. As it was not, the other eye ended up being overtaxed, and as a result has gradually weakened. The patient has been relying mainly on her left eye when viewing objects up close, particularly when reading. Not at all unusual in such circumstances. Over the years, the hypermetropia of the right eye has increased, as was to be expected. The eye becomes teary, causes headaches, weakness . . . even anxiety attacks. Do you understand?"

24

Of course I understood. I tried to understand everything that happened between Kati and me, to find the red, no, the golden thread on which I could string all the events from our very first lunch together. And yet I often think back to Kati's words during that lunch. "But we won't ask each other any questions," she had said, and I still remember how my senses had reeled, as I felt she was offering me her hand on a rope strung high in the air on which the two of us, lone tight-rope walkers, teetered above the world that lay far below.

"What's going on here?" I heard Baleli ask, as she finally turned and looked at me.

As usual, she had arrived unannounced. As usual, she had smiled at me as I opened the door, had waited for me to come up to her, bend forward to her hair, lay my hands on her shoulders, almost push her through the door, and then follow her through the front hall. As usual, I walked behind the most elegant and irreproachable woman that I had ever met in my life – the essence of good taste and style. And as usual, I could not tear my eyes from the long, light-red braid swaying over her back. For an instant I felt as if nothing at all had changed in my life.

"What's going on here?" she repeated, peering at me with her slightly slanted green eyes. I realized there was nowhere for her to sit. I looked around. The piano room was completely unrecognizable. The piano no longer stood against the wall as before, but was now in the middle of the room facing the balcony. The sofa had landed in the kitchen, where it turned out to be far more practical, and in its stead Kati had set up a kind of "lying-and-listening" area with the Turkish carpets that she and I had bought, and blue cushions, among which lay a few books, a basket of fruit, Kati's thick stockings, and an empty glass. The chandelier that had hung from the centre of the ceiling had been moved to hang over this new den. The only room in the flat that had remained more or less unchanged, that had somehow, by some higher grace, escaped Kati's systematic propagation of anarchy, or rather her new order, was my study. Even dust, which until Kati's arrival I had almost forgotten existed, and which as a result of her unsystematic battle with it had settled over the whole flat as if it had fallen from heaven, had by some miracle avoided my study.

I nodded at the piano stool for Baleli to sit on, and smiled in spite of myself.

"What does Ema say about all of this?" she asked, pulling the piano stool towards her.

"Nothing," I replied. I did not want to talk about Ema.

She sat down, crossed her flawless legs, and leaned back against the piano. I sat down in front of her on the floor, and leaned back against the wall.

"You're alone?"

"Yes, I am. Kati is taking an exercise class. She always takes exercise classes on Thursdays – Thursdays from seven to nine."

"I see," she said, nodding her head. "And what about you?" she added after a pause.

"Me? I don't take exercise classes."

"I can imagine you don't. Well, till now you never have. But with you one never knows, does one?" she said with a touch of bitterness in her voice, and looked around the room again.

She was tanned, as she always was in summer. And like all redheads, the skin of her face, neck, and the area above her orange, low-cut *cache-coeur* was covered with countless light-brown freckles. Baleli definitely carries her fifty years extremely well . . . no, her fifty-six years . . . Only her hands betray her, I said to myself, and thought of Kati's hands.

"You look a little pale, Tibor," she said, also studying me. "Are you taking your blood pressure pills?"

My blood pressure pills . . . I tried to discern whether she was making fun of me, or if she simply had not managed to cast her habit of looking after me aside.

"Ema told me that you're not," she answered for me. "And that ever since, well . . . ever since you're no longer alone, you haven't touched them. At least not while she was still here."

"Ema?"

"Yes, Ema," she continued, her voice normal. "She came out to the country to help me clean The Molehill. Like she does every summer. We aired the whole place, took out the carpets and blankets, polished the furniture, chased the ants out of the kitchen, changed the sheets in your bedroom, turned over the earth in the rose beds behind the house, and watered the lawn and your strawberries."

She rummaged around in her basket – for as long as I have known her, she has always carried a small wicker basket instead of a handbag.

"I brought you the keys, Tibor," she said in a low voice. "A few days in Picardy will do you good, and also your . . . what was her name again . . . Kati? I can't believe you didn't think of it yourself. Simon will drop by towards the end of the week, after his concert in Brussels."

25

Of course. Picardy. The Somme, slowly flowing by. Birds twittering. The sparkle of their little white bellies in the sun. The endless expanse of the dunes. The low-hanging haze. The rosy sand. The nocturnal sighing of the ocean. The cool linen sheets. My walnut-wood bed. Why had I not thought of Picardy?

In Picardy we will finally love one another . . . I felt a tremor in my stomach and my temples, and had to sit down. All this time that Kati was locking herself in the semicircular room with the cupola . . . tiptoeing back home late at night . . .

running around the flat half-dressed . . . chatting to me in the bathroom, still damp from her morning shower . . . trying on her clothes in front of me, asking my advice . . . sitting on my lap . . . even pressing herself close to me, bending over my shoulder so that I could feel the pressure of those two little animals of hers against me . . . at times opening her legs, her inner thighs trembling . . . yet turning to stone whenever my hand reached out to her. She turns her head away when I try to kiss her on the lips. She rolls herself into a ball when I caress her stomach. Her head starts aching the instant she feels my breath on her.

"The Molehill?" she asked, taken aback, when I suggested we go to Picardy.

The Molehill is a house by the sea, not far from the village of Saint Valéry. Baleli and I had bought it during our first and only year of marriage. I had sold my book *Late Strawberries*, and Baleli had sold a set of Louis XVI chairs and her favourite late-eighteenth-century chest of drawers. I no longer remember why I had called the house "The Molehill", since it is big and filled with light and has two narrow towers, seven rooms, and a large, square kitchen. When Baleli and I separated, we had no reason to want to separate ourselves from the house. Baleli continued busying herself with it, collecting an incredibly diverse selection of knick-knacks, furniture, carpets, and mirrors, which in time gave the house its inimitable Balelian stamp. I would usually go there during the week, at times with Marie-Hélène when we were finishing a book, at times with some other woman with whom I did not necessarily intend to do business, and most times alone when I wanted to be alone. Towards the end of the week Baleli's antique-dealer friends began showing up in Picardy, along with Farkas and his group, and from time to time even Simon Osterman, if he happened to be between operas or concerts.

Kati clapped her hands together enthusiastically.

"Yes, let's go!" she said. And the very same day we rented a car. Kati gathered up our clothes, even ironed a few of my shirts, which in the past I had always taken to the drycleaners, and placed our pyjamas one on top of the other. She bought herself a straw hat, and piled everything into a single suitcase.

When the next morning we headed up north along the *autoroute* in a chartreuse Citroen, when we gazed at the plains and the monochrome sky, when I turned to look at her from time to time, her arms happily dancing, when she patted my knee, when I thought about our shared suitcase in the boot of the car and our pyjamas lying on top of one another, when I lit myself a cigarette and sucked in the first, deep drag of smoke – I told myself . . . what did I tell myself? No, if I'm not mistaken it was not so much a question of words but of a feeling, a nascent presentiment that before us lay a road that was short, intense and dangerous, and that beyond that road lay a different life, a very different life indeed.

26

Every good novel, I always told Farkas, toys with illusion, with an *idée fixe* that it attempts to develop to an extreme. That is why Agathe had to die – in Jacob's arms, no less – and that is why the initial drop of blood that trickled from Agathe's nose to her lips proved to be a lethal wound, a fatal well, a red flower on a summer dress. That is why Lorenzo Bosco ultimately has to leave Anna – she is the one who has initiated his rebirth, and yet he cannot begin his new life with her, he must start anew. Farkas told me that I am ruthless, that I am a tyrant, a terrorist, that I am always insisting on formulas and definitions, always having to be in control . . . maybe you're right, I replied, but the same blood that flows in life also flows in novels, a novel is concentrated life, gathering its tributaries, driving them towards the rapids, damming them up, slowing them to a stop, pouring them into deltas – a novel gives shape to the shapeless, seeks hidden formulas . . . What do you mean, hidden formulas? Farkas did not like my digressions, either in my writing or in myself, he told me, adding that as the years went by I was becoming increasingly irritating and obsessive, prepared only to listen to the sound of my own voice and to head in the direction I had chosen . . . You can call this formula by any name you want, I said to him: triangle of celestial bodies . . . lines on the palm of a hand . . . the mechanism of a clock . . .

The first thing, or rather the first human being, we saw, when the chartreuse Citroen pulled up crackling over the gravel in front of The Molehill, was Farkas. He was lying on my red-and-yellow deckchair with a newspaper, apparently waiting for us. Kati and I exchanged a quick glance. Her eyes were alert and clear, like an icy mountain lake. She pushed down hard on the handle and opened the car door. So we will not be alone after all, I said to myself, and got out of the car. Farkas clapped me on the back. "Finally you've brought her out into the world, you son of a lion!" he murmured. "Now we'll get a chance to look at her too!"

Farkas, a very intuitive man, could not have put it better. In Picardy, in the light or through the eyes of others, I would see a new Katarina-Kati-Grushenka. Very different from the Kati I had taken home in a taxi that first night, with whom I had walked under the acacia trees on the avenue Carnot and sat on the sofa in the kitchen. From the Kati who watched me shave in the morning, with whom I went to order glasses, and who had packed our shared suitcase. In Picardy, with Baleli, Farkas and his wife, Pablo – an actor and also quite a collector (I had included him in my novel *The New New Héloïse*) – his daughter Ludmila, and later Simon Osterman, I discovered quite a few things. That Kati is unusually adaptable, in other words she can be either conventional or superficial when required. That she is able, quite seamlessly, to take things in hand – a conversation at the dinner table, for instance, or the organization of an afternoon or evening. That she has a sense of humour that is reflective, and which while nimble, has a streak of darkness in it. That she is a true polyglot: besides French, which, as I was convinced from the day we met, was not her mother tongue, she also speaks Italian, German, and Spanish, a fact that stunned everyone else as much as it did me. That she is a liar: when Pablo asked her at table what she does, or rather how she fills her days, she told him that she is studying "revisionist" geography and history. "Personal history and geography," she had then added. That she is terrified of bats: there are a few families of bats living in the labyrinth of discarded furniture, china, and other odds and ends up in The Molehill's attic. That she is an excellent dancer, a fact I will come back to later. That she likes all men's eyes to be on her. That she is a seductress. That she is a . . .

More about that later. About our single day in Picardy and the long night that followed. In Picardy I began to approach what I have summed up as the hidden formula. At times I am deeply dissatisfied with myself, because I have the tendency, even now that I am almost sixty, of focusing on all kinds of detail. That there are certain things I cannot express with precision and simplicity. As in the final sentence of *Wild Palms*, which never ceases to perturb me: "If I am to choose between nothingness and sorrow, then my choice will be sorrow." The novel serves as a path to this realization.

27

Simon Osterman arrived that evening. He came in through the French doors that open out onto the garden. Kati and Pablo were busy moving aside the table and chairs, as everyone except me wanted to dance. Farkas was riffling through my record collection. Kati had put on a pale-yellow taffeta gown with black flowers, cinched at the waist and ruffled out, and very low-cut at the back. She had put up her hair in a high coiffure, and was wearing the black bee-shaped earrings we had bought in a boutique not far from the Anatolian carpet-merchant's shop. Her cheeks were slightly flushed. I noticed bright ringlets by her ears and her temples. She had never before struck me as so exceptionally beautiful.

We all turned towards the wide-open French doors when we heard steps on the terrace. Then Simon Osterman stood before us as if he had fallen out of the night sky, the sleeves of his white shirt rolled up, a large leather bag hanging from his shoulder. He was out of breath, visibly exhausted after his long drive, but with the captivating smile on his lips that I knew so well.

"Simon!" Baleli called out excitedly, and hurried over to take his heavy bag. Apparently she had not expected him to come so late, nor had she expected him to come through the French doors.

"What are you all up to?" he asked, looking at us one by one in astonishment.

"Kati feels like dancing," Farkas said.

"I do?" Kati asked, taken aback. It had been Farkas's idea, even if Kati and the others had no objections. Simon turned to her slowly and intently.

"Have you already chosen your partner?" he asked, rolling down his sleeves.

Kati ran her hands down her forearms, as if she were mirroring Simon.

"To be perfectly honest, I have been waiting for you," she almost whispered.

There was a short silence. Farkas took a record out of the pile.

"Why don't you tell us what your orchestra played in Brussels," I said in an attempt to change the subject.

Simon walked over to Kati. "*Verklärte Nacht*," he said to her more than to me. And then almost as an echo, "*Transfigured Night . . . La Notte trasfigurata . . . La nuit transfigurée*."

Of course, of course, I thought with growing helplessness, and looked out of the window into the late-summer night. Simon is one of the masters of Schoenberg – no one can conduct *Transfigured Night* the way Simon Osterman does, even if this sounds somewhat pompous. He conducts *Transfigured Night* like a long, intense, fiery spasm, like a convulsion of joy and pain, like . . . like an orgasm. A shudder ran down my spine. Like a woman's orgasm, I thought, and felt a dull pain in my temples.

"What's wrong with you, Tibor?" Baleli asked.

"Nothing, nothing at all . . . I'm going to smoke a cigarette. Outside . . ." I mumbled.

"Do you want me to come with you?" she asked.

I shook my head, and went out through the main door.

Outside I was enveloped by the thick and humid night. We might even have some rain, I thought. One of those sudden summer storms. I smelt the sea, and then heard the distant sighs of its rolling waves. I looked at the moon that had hidden behind the poplars. I moved so that I could see its narrow face, and lit a cigarette. I sucked in the first deep drag of smoke. I walked down the lawn beside the fence. This cigarette is going to help me gather my thoughts, I said to myself. Thoughts that were colliding like billiard balls. Simon Osterman – Kati – Irina, Simon's first wife, a harpist, yes, a harpist with a long neck – the letter beneath the mattress – Bianca, Bianca – the red car – the Belgian lorry carrying live-stock – Bianca's throaty laugh – Simon's bare forearms – Kati's pale yellow silk taffeta gown – the ringlets by her temples, which I had only noticed today – the pyjamas in our shared suitcase – the linen sheets of my bed – *Verklärte Nacht* – To be perfectly honest . . . Kati would like to dance – What did you play in Brussels? – To be perfectly honest . . . I have been waiting for you.

I continued walking on the lawn through the garden. I

threw away my cigarette and turned to look back. Through the bright windows came the faraway sound of music. Light music. Italian, I thought. I quickly started walking back. God knows why I suddenly wanted to see them. I stopped behind the final poplar near the house. Now I could hear the music quite well: it wasn't Italian, but a lithe and lively jazz.

I leaned against the poplar and looked through the open French doors: Kati's yellow dress with the black flowers was twirling, whirling, and falling again, resting for a few sudden beats of soft, melodic jazz. Her hair flickered in the air. Her bare feet hardly touched the ground. Her hands were holding Pablo's. Yes, Pablo was holding both her hands, spinning her around, pulling her close, pushing her away, twirling her in a pirouette, letting go of her for a slower step, grabbing hold of her again . . . Simon stood leaning against the wall, his arms crossed, watching her like I was.

So Kati-Katarina-Grushenka is an excellent dancer.

I lit another cigarette.

28

Picardy, which I have always loved – the remoteness, the non-Frenchness, the rare birds, the cafés decorated in the worst possible taste, the long sandy beaches where one's murkiest thoughts find clarity, the fishing village on the Somme, and even the provincials on their Sunday walk – became for me in a single evening and night a terrible nightmare.

When I returned to the house, after a short walk on the beach and a couple of cigarettes that helped clear my thoughts, there wasn't a single trace of jazz left. The table and chairs were back in their places, and only the wall-light over the armchair where Farkas sat reading was on.

"Where is everyone?" I asked him.

Farkas looked at me with his penetrating, fox-like eyes, and ran his fingers over his pencil moustache.

"Baleli is asleep in her room. And so is Ludmila. Pablo . . ."

"What about Kati?" I asked.

"Kati and Simon are out on the beach," he replied.

I sat down in the armchair opposite him. I felt my thighs trembling and the blood draining from my face. I looked at my hands and tried to remember one of the magic spells from my childhood. As a boy, and later as a young man, I tried to wish myself away when I found myself in a critical situation. To extricate myself, to escape from my body and see myself from a distance, as if I were someone else. If I had looked at myself from a distance then, it would have been from Farkas's armchair, and the situation, no matter how critical, would have taken on a completely different aspect. But the more I groped among the old spells that in the past had freed me from difficult situations, the more clearly I saw before me nothing but myself, R. A. Tibor (as Baleli would say), crushed and dismayed; and the more clearly I saw that the dismay was not simply because R. A. Tibor was not spending the night in the company of his Kati-Katarina-Grushenka, as he had imagined in the chartreuse Citroen. Nor that she was spending the night with someone else – after all, this wouldn't be the first time. But rather it was because that other man, his friend, his special friend, was the last man on earth he would want for her.

My God, I thought and buried my face in my hands, who would have thought that I would ever be thinking along these lines: a man that I would want for her.

I felt Farkas eyeing me from behind his book.

"Aren't you going to bed, Tibor?" he asked with concern.

I shook my head. Lightning flashed beyond the French doors, followed by thunder.

"Ha! Rain!" Farkas said, getting up. "Good night, you son of a lion."

He is still calling me "son of a lion"! How many times have I told him to stop calling me "son of a lion", to curb this zoological passion of his. At least where I am concerned. As it is, I feel like I am his racehorse. Somewhat exhausted and worn out after all these years. And yet still the racehorse that Farkas has been backing from the very beginning, and which, for better or worse, he is prepared to go on backing.

Another flash of lightning, thunder. Then came the violent downpour. Water pounded the French doors and fell crashing onto the terrace. I thought of Kati's silk taffeta gown. About her bare arms that had struck me as too long at the optician's. That she would get wet and catch a chill. I shuddered. I looked around the room. Baleli's jacket was lying on the sofa.

I wrapped it around my shoulders and looked out into the night again. I wanted to wait for her, even if I had to wait until morning.

29

"Is it about your heart?" Eli Benjamin's voice came over the phone. He was the doctor who monitored the rise and fall of my blood pressure, always warning me against cardinal complications. Cardiac complications, he would correct me. Cardinal, I would repeat. A cardiac complication can only be cardinal, doctor. Full stop, the end, the curtain falls. You're right, you're right, all the more reason why you should carefully follow my regimen, he always replied.

Eli Benjamin, a shy young generalist, who besides medicine also has a passion for astrophysics, had sent me a letter a few years earlier about Agathe, or rather about her astrophysical theories. He wrote in a narrow, cramped hand, telling me that he had been gripped by my novel, particularly the ending, which he had not expected – her dying like that on the street, at a table on a café terrace in the arms of the young man who had in fact caused her death – but that he could not accept Agathe's astrophysical theories, which were not only dubious from a scientific standpoint, but also quite far-fetched. The idea of a supernova manifesting itself in the middle of the day at the moment of Agathe's death might be highly poetic, but it is completely preposterous. I do not know why I answered his letter; perhaps because of his cramped handwriting and that signature, which with its three lines was like a sketch of his face. His face was in reality somewhat longish, with even lips and slanted eyes. We met at a café near Farkas's office, and later even had lunch together. He gave me his business card, and from that day on became my personal physician.

"No, it's not about my heart," I replied late in the afternoon on the day after our evening and night in Picardy, though I could just as well have answered in the affirmative – Kati was bound so closely to my heart, and I was calling him about her.

When I had woken on the old sofa that morning, covered by Baleli's jacket, it had already been day for quite a while. One of those beautiful clear summer days that follow storms. I went out into the garden. The grass was still wet from the rain. I looked in front of the house where the chartreuse Citroen stood. But where was Simon's car?

"Simon has left," Baleli told me, as I came back into the house. She was making coffee and turned her back to me.

"What about Kati?" I asked, holding my breath.

"She's asleep."

She was sleeping in my bed, between the linen sheets. The sheets were pulled up all the way to her chin. Her forehead was hot and her cheeks were flushed. Her yellow gown lay wet and crumpled on my desk.

We left the same morning. Kati was shivering with cold, and had dark rings under her eyes.

"I'll call the doctor when we get to Paris," I said absently.

"I've lost one of my bees," she murmured.

"One of your bees?"

"My earring."

That was all we said during our ride back to Paris.

Eli Benjamin came over towards evening. I took him to the semicircular room and left the two of them alone. I waited for him in my study.

"I don't know what is wrong with your . . ."

"Kati."

"But she does have a high fever. And I am afraid that it might well get higher," he said and, as he shook my hand at the door, added, "I wouldn't worry though. Sometimes a fever can be beneficial."

30

What was it he said? Beneficial? The following day, when Kati was ill and trembling with cold, so that I no longer knew what to cover her with, though at the same time she was burning with fever, a popular science magazine sent me a questionnaire which, according to the few lines of introduction, was being sent to a handful of authors who "have a particular feel for the human soul in its various manifestations", and who might be able "to shed some light from a different angle on the subject at hand: happiness". The questionnaire consisted of just one question: "In your opinion, what is happiness?"

I think I need not stress that under normal circumstances I would never have responded to an initiative of this kind.

But Kati's illness was not a normal circumstance.

During those days that began with Eli Benjamin's visit, time and space started wavering as though in a hurricane. Time was no longer made up of hours flowing one after another, forming the first day, the second. Time was not the tracking of the sun and its daily revolution. Time became Kati's skin upon mine, the sweat that oozed from it, her damp hair that fell on my face, her hands that gripped me and frantically caressed my temples, her bloated stomach, the yoghurt that she managed to eat, the tea that she finally managed to drink. Space was the conical cupola that I stared up at as at a new sky.

"Tibor . . . Don't leave me alone!" she cried, as I showed Eli Benjamin out. I returned over the arterial balcony to the semicircular room with the cupola. She was lying the wrong way around on the bed, curled up into a ball, her head where her feet usually lay, the blanket pulled up to her ears. I picked up her dress, which was lying on the floor. The one with the red tulips. The jacket she had worn with it. Her pants, her panties. Books piled one on top of the other, papers. Even a shrivelled piece of fruit. What an incredibly messy little girl she is, I said to myself, and was taken aback – it was the first time I had ever referred to her as a little girl.

"Tibor, lie down next to me," she whispered from under the covers.

Had I heard right?

I went over to the bed and sat down on the edge.

"Come close to me."

I glanced at the spindly rootless plant that had flourished since she had brought it into the house. I bent down to untie my shoelaces. I felt my heart pound.

"No, no . . . forget your shoes . . . take off your shirt . . ."

"Kati," I whispered more to myself than to her, and straightened up.

She raised the covers. Her body lay before me, within reach. She was wearing nothing but a pair of ridiculous underpants that were far too large. I gazed at the slim shoulders, the shoulders of a long-distance swimmer, at her breasts, pressing together like two small white sheep, a chocolate-brown beauty spot on one of them, at her taut, bloated stomach, at her navel, a dark button. For an instant I closed my eyes to the honey-coloured brightness of her skin. It was only when I opened them again that I noticed that her body was trembling, shuddering with fever and cold. I seized the cover and pulled it towards me. She embraced me tightly and entwined her legs with mine. I unbuttoned my shirt, took it off, and dropped it on the floor. I rolled onto my back and pulled her onto me. I felt the weight of her body on mine. The pressure of those two small sheep of hers. Her hair spilled over my face. Her face pressed against mine, I could hear her teeth chatter.

"Kati, Kati," I said over and over.

"I feel cold, Tibor. I feel so cold," she whispered into my ear.

I pressed her harder against me.

"But you're so hot," I said, caressing her back.

"Cold . . . cold," she repeated.

I do not know how long we remained like this, our bodies entangled. I remember that the grip of her hands slowly relaxed, that her teeth stopped chattering, and that she became increasingly heavy. She's asleep, I said to myself, carefully removing her hair from my eyes. I wiped her sweating brow with the edge of the coverlet. With my tongue I felt my way over the skin of her shoulders – smooth, soft, sticky, salty, sweetly salty. I did not move. I do not know how long I lay there without moving. After a while I could no longer feel my right arm, and a sharp pain throbbed in my lower back. I also began feeling hot, and our mingled sweat trickled from between our stomachs. Now and then Kati started like a frightened animal, almost sliding out of my arms. She even moaned a few words I did not understand. Perhaps I too fell asleep for a few moments. Yes, it is possible that I sank into a silent, fleeting sleep, and that I was awakened by moans in an unknown tongue.

31

But that's Russian she's speaking, I said to myself. She is speaking Russian in those teeth-chattering dreams of hers. Or perhaps some other Slavic language. Slovene, for instance, which I didn't even know existed until recently. I gently laid the arm I could still feel around her shoulders. To be perfectly honest, at that moment I did not care in the least what language she was dreaming in – Russian, Slovene, Bulgarian. The thing that I did care about, that I cared about more than anything in the world, was her feverish body lying on mine, abandoned, slippery, trembling, reeking of spoiled shellfish, and also my willingness to continue lying there beneath her.

I knew that we had to do something, that we had to stop the fever. Aspirin, cold water, beetroot juice, Eli Benjamin . . . I mulled over the possibilities.

Kati opened her eyes as if she had heard me. We looked at one another. Her eyes were burning, like her body. I wanted to kiss her, her feverish eyes, her mouth, those two pretty little sheep of hers, her wet stomach. But instead of kissing her I pushed her away. I was suddenly in a hurry, a great hurry. I got up, walked to the bathroom in the dark, and began to fill the tub with lukewarm water. Then I went to get Kati. I lifted her in my arms like a child and carried her to the bathroom. I took off the ridiculous underpants she was wearing.

"They're not underpants, they're pyjamas . . ." she mumbled, and sat down on the edge of the tub. Her triangle was as honey-coloured as her hair. Chestnuts and honey. When she lay down in the tub, her triangle absorbed the water and turned a dark, lustreless, pearly colour. I washed her face. I lathered her body with a facecloth. I bent down over her pearly triangle. This was definitely no time for such things, yet I felt my hands tremble. She closed her eyes and abandoned herself to the water. I wanted to wash her hair.

"No, no . . . my head . . ." she moaned.

"I'll just rinse your hair a little," I insisted.

After I did wash and rinse her hair I left her alone for a few moments. I went to the kitchen and prepared a yoghurt drink and got a piece of buttered bread and two aspirins. I changed the sheets on her bed. I aired the semicircular room with the cupola. Then I dried her and wrapped her in my bathrobe. She laid her head on my shoulder. She looked soft and calm. I took her back to the semicircular room. I tried to find a new pair of pyjamas in all the mess. Then I went and got her a pair of mine. I helped her put them on. The two little sheep huddled timidly inside. She looked at me almost incredulously. She climbed into the freshly made bed. I felt her forehead. She still had a fever. Perhaps a little less now. Yes, definitely a degree or two less. I brought her the yoghurt drink. She turned to the other side and pulled the covers over her head. I don't know why, but it got into my head that she had to have something in her stomach. If not the piece of buttered bread, then at least some yoghurt. In the end she did drink it. First with little sips, then she finished the whole glass. I stroked her hair. It was damp, but soft and no longer sticky. I sat down on the edge of the bed and took her hand in mine. She did not pull it away but continued to look at me with her sparkling eyes. Her hand as it lay in mine seemed helpless and smaller than it really was. And whiter. Her nails still cut like those of a child. I turned her hand over and looked at her palm as if I could read it. For a second I felt as if I could. Its first line, the one beginning at the base of the fingers, the heart line, which at the start of its course emerged from a countless tangle of little islands, flowing clearly and smoothly, surely indicated the point at which she had met me.

Later, when she had fallen into a long, deep, healing sleep, and I found the questionnaire lying on my desk, I picked up my pen, and without a moment's thought wrote: "Happiness is a bout of high fever."

32

Kati's convalescence, which brought with it a return of regular time and space, and in a sense a natural flow of events, began at exactly three-thirty the following afternoon, the windiest day of the whole summer, definitely heralding its demise.

"Where's that wind coming from?" were Kati's first words after her stormy fever subsided.

I turned and looked at her. Her eyes were calm and filled with astonishment, as if they had come back from afar. Her skin had regained its honeyed hue. How many hours had she slept? Ten, fifteen? I, too, had slept my fill. To tell the truth, it had been a long time since I had slept so well as that night, or rather that morning, in the wrought-iron bed. As I awoke I felt the scent of her hair in my nostrils. I moved closer – her breath was regular, calm, and she smelled once more of peaches. I turned onto my back and for a while lay motionless next to her. Then I quietly got out of bed and drew the covers over her. I made myself a cup of coffee in the kitchen. I hadn't been so hungry in ages. It wasn't surprising – it was midday already, and I could not remember when I had last eaten. I went to buy bread, milk, cheese, croissants, and bananas. Madame Cipriani, whom I had badgered all summer about Benz's disappearance, returned my greeting for the first time in a long while. I ate breakfast, took a shower, put on some fresh clothes, and settled down with a book in the armchair at the foot of Kati's bed.

And so she woke up in surprise. Never before had she asked me as many questions as she did during her first day of convalescence. All kinds of questions: about the afternoon wind, about my dark-red pyjamas with black stripes that she had woken up in, about her illness which had taken her aback with its force, about Brahms – why did Lorenzo Bosco love Brahms with such passion, where had I met Baleli, and about destiny – did I believe in destiny, or were destiny and free will as incompatible as we imagined, and did I think that destiny had anything to do with God.

I suggested we play cards. Rummy or canasta are perfect games for the first day of one's convalescence, I explained. In one of my desk drawers I found some old waxed cards (in actual fact Farkas's) with a Persian-carpet design on their backs, and did my very best to answer her questions. From time to time we glanced at each other over the tops of our cards. Kati played with extreme seriousness, knitting her brow at her hand and shaking her head, all the while listening to me attentively.

A cold wind towards the end of August – on the twenty-eighth to be exact – that shakes the few trees lining the rue Balzac with such vigour is nothing out of the ordinary. One day in mid-June, during my second Parisian summer, thirty-three years ago, the sky had suddenly grown dark and it had begun to hail. Within minutes the pavements were covered with walnut-sized marbles of ice. Children threw them into the air and passers-by crushed them beneath their feet. Her illness had also taken *me* aback. What had caused the fever? Eli Benjamin had told me that it was most likely viral in nature. Although there were also cases, in his experience, of individuals who somehow initiated their own fever. In any case, it was over now. My dark-red pyjamas looked as if they were made for her. The sleeves were obviously too long, as were the pants. But that deep wine colour next to the honeyed hue of her skin. Brahms? No, I did not want to talk about Brahms. Brahms and Lorenzo Bosco were linked with Simon. And I did not want to talk about Simon today. I was prepared to talk about anything or anybody, but not about Simon Osterman. So I failed to hear the question about Simon and stared at my cards. I was missing the Queen of Hearts. I had met Baleli at an auction. At an auction? Back then? Back when? Before you met Baleli. Yes, I used to like going to auctions back then. I would sit among the buyers and other onlookers and listen. Yes, I would listen. For me auctions were more than anything else a matter of listening. Of rhythm, silence, tension, sudden acceleration, quivering voices, leaps into the void, into the unknown, the liberation of the auction hammer . . . Seventeen thousand, seventeen thousand two hundred, seventeen thousand three hundred . . . seventeen thousand seven hundred . . . Her voice had been like polished crystal. Clean, clear, sharp as a blade. I turned and looked in her direction. Élisabeth Béranger was a young woman with a long, proud neck, slanted green eyes, and a thick braid of light-red hair that hung over her breast. Had she not bitten her lower lip, from under which flashed strong, healthy teeth, I would perhaps not have waited for her by the door. Kati, it's your turn . . . Tell me more, Tibor . . . Her deformed lip . . . I felt an irrepressible desire to kiss that beautiful redhead on the lips, and to save her lower lip. Just that, nothing else. But Élisabeth Béranger wanted everything: marriage, children, furniture, silver cutlery, a tea service, a coffee service, ornate sugar tongs . . . Free will and destiny? Had Baleli not bitten her lower lip at that very moment, I would most probably never have had the desire to kiss her face with its severe beauty that inspired fear, even anxiety. But Baleli read our kiss on the pont Alexandre III as a sure sign of destiny. Free will and destiny are probably different names for one and the same thing – the stream into which we fall and which carries us away. God has nothing to do with either the one or the other, and at the same time everything. For God is but another name for man within man. O Kati!

33

I gazed at the faces in front of me: an elderly woman in a straw hat who was nervously clenching her hands. A youth chewing gum. A man in a grey coat, with a gold bracelet and hairy hands. A woman with the jaw of a glutton. The bus is my laboratory. Number 31, Place de l'Étoile–Gare du Nord, the window seat behind the driver, from which I can see all the seats facing mine. In the bus my thoughts are at their lightest and most daring. When I do not know how to continue with a chapter I have begun, when I begin repeating myself, when I am searching for a new idea, when my intuition fails me, when my eyes glaze over, that is when I get on a bus. As I did this afternoon. The bus was just turning into the narrow rue Guy Moquet when it began to rain. Heavy drops trickled down the window past my face.

I tried to run through my mind the events of the last few hours – meticulously, one after the other, not missing the slightest detail that might well reveal more than one would have first thought. I wanted to understand what had led to the sudden change, the scene that had erupted between the two of us, in which Simon Osterman was somehow involved. We had played cards almost the whole afternoon until it got dark and we had to turn on the lights. Kati was completely immersed in the game, even though she was asking me a whole series of questions, so that I almost felt as if I were telling her fairy tales. Like the one about the beautiful redhead, daughter of the renowned Paris lawyer Xavier Béranger, who lived on the bank of the Seine, Quai de Conti, and who loved objects with a passion – chairs, armchairs, commodes, desks, cups, teapots – and who some day would perhaps open the best, or at least the most intriguing antique shop one could imagine. Then one day, while she was attending one of her weekly auctions, she met a man a few years older than her, with unruly light-chestnut hair and a self-assured smile, who waited for her by the door with his hands in his pockets.

Kati pensively held her cards to her breasts. I reached out my hand. I took the cards out of her hand and laid them on the floor. My God! When I think back, how ridiculous it all was, how tasteless. My hand with its bulging veins and brownish spots. My hand, increasingly bold on her immaculate torso that glowed from beneath the pyjama vest. She suddenly grabbed my hand and pushed me away. I felt the ruthless, effervescing power of her body and my body's blind, adamant, hot-headed desire, which not only hardened in the pit of my stomach but spread everywhere, to my arms, my legs, my face, and even my eyes.

"Tibor! Get away from me!" she hissed through clenched teeth.

I removed my hands and laid my head on her stomach. She tried to wriggle out from under me, to free herself from the weight of my head. I caught her wrists and pressed them down hard against the mattress. I wanted, by fair means or foul, to keep my head resting against her stomach. We fought, panting and silent. I want my head on her stomach, on her stomach, I kept saying to myself, and tried with all my might to subdue her writhing body. Suddenly the tension in her muscles relaxed. Her stomach sank beneath me as if it were bottomless. The following moment my whole body was shaken by an abrupt spasm, and without my feeling the slightest rapture discharged a stream of warm, milky liquid.

Kati raised her head from the bed and freed her arms. She closed her eyes and began breathing through her mouth. I too closed my eyes and breathed through my mouth. When I opened my eyes again and raised my head from her stomach, it was already evening.

"I would like to sleep, Tibor," she said, and then added, "alone."

When I woke the following day she was already up and fully dressed, her hair neat – she was even wearing makeup.

"What is going on?" I asked her, looking at her with bleary eyes.

"Nothing," she answered with a smile.

I sat down on the ornate sofa, which in the past had stood by the piano. She was wearing the dress with the red tulips. Her hair was tied back with a black velvet ribbon. Her face was pale, she had lost weight during her illness, and yet she was prettier. Yes, the illness has made her prettier, I said to myself.

"Where are you going?" I suddenly asked her.

"Out."

"Out?" I was astonished.

She folded her arms and looked at me as if I had just said the most foolish thing imaginable. The thought that she had probably arranged a rendezvous with Simon tore through me like an electric shock. Simon liked making love in the morning. He always said that women are ready to slip between his sheets at the break of day: the first violinist, the flutist, some soprano or other from the chorus, Olga van B, a forty-four-year-old journalist from Rotterdam who is writing a book on conductors and dutifully waits for him in the lobby of every hotel – in Vienna, Glasgow, Brussels, Lille, Milan, Palermo, a long-legged, andrygenous hairdresser. It's either in the morning or you can forget it, he used to say. After sex he always took a shower. O the sweet gush of the shower, he would say. And after the shower, the day began. His days and his evenings were dedicated to one thing and one thing only – beginning with “mu” and ending with “ic”. Do you understand me, Tibor? Do you? It’s either in the morning, or you can forget it, I murmured to myself.

“What did you say?” she asked me.

I turned away from her and walked to the front door. I double-locked it and dropped the key into my pocket. Kati watched me from the far side of the hall.

“You’re not going anywhere,” I told her with calm decisiveness. “A day and a half after your fever! Where’s your logic?”

“It didn’t drop into your pocket, like yours just did! Open the door!” she shouted.

“Kati . . .” I began, intending to calm her.

“Grushenka!” she corrected me angrily, throwing up her arms.

“Katarina. Kati . . . you know that I’m only thinking of what’s best for you,” I said.

She laughed out loud. She sat on the floor, took off her shoes, and, still laughing, threw first one at me and then the other.

I wanted to stay on the bus for another circuit. To think everything through one more time: my ejaculating into the void, the sharp pain that came with it, the anxiety and the shame, the sepulchral silence between us . . . Was she aware of what had happened? What did her laughter in the hall signify?

I heard steps behind me and the nasal, admonishing voice of the driver, “Last stop, Monsieur.”

34

From two until three, or possibly three-thirty is the worst period of the night. Until two there is still hope that I might fall asleep, that for me sleep might come late, but with a healing power, taking me under its wing. By three-thirty, however, when darkness is at its densest, day is already beginning to stir. Bus, Métro, and taxi drivers, workers, writers – those who write in the morning – turn on the lights in their flats. At four-thirty, buses begin running down my avenue, buses number 68 and 135. At five, Monsieur Jansen from the second floor takes his dog Jenny for a walk. They head for the Palais Rothschild and disappear around the corner of the rue du Faubourg Saint-Honoré. They reappear again on the rue Balzac some fifteen minutes later. Jenny meekly stops in front of our house door and waits for Monsieur Jansen to open the door.

But from two until three, or possibly three-thirty, I am alone in this world. Banished, exiled from sleeping humanity. That one-and-a-half hours is my dark ravine. In its merciless abyss I stand face to face with myself. Its cold walls offer no escape. R. A. Tibor standing before R. A. Tibor, as Baleli would say. How can I escape myself? How can I, at least for a few redeeming hours, forget myself? When the last streetlamp goes out in the neighbouring avenue, when I no longer hear the footsteps of some nocturnal pedestrian, my only brother, when anguish and extreme exhaustion clutch at my throat, I reach beneath my pillow. Morphylon, Hupovan, Noctalia . . . these are the names of my hated saviours. For a few hours, they plunge me into oblivion. Life is not an uninterrupted line. Tomorrow another day will begin.

From two until three, and at times three-thirty . . . At five Monsieur Jansen and Jenny appear. From the semicircular room with the cupola I can see them walk down the rue Balzac. Kati turns in her bed and sighs in her morning sleep. Kati has changed not only my days, but also my nights. From two until three and, drop by drop, until three-thirty, is always the deepest period of the night. The ravine, the abyss . . . only now I no longer stare at my own countenance, at the murky depths within me and at the unwavering process of decay which we call life. Kati stands where my reflection appears in the mirror of the night. Wherever I look, I see her. When I close my eyes, I see her sauntering past me. Back and forth before my eyes . . . Kati in a warm bath . . . Kati with her new glasses . . . Kati in her yellow silk taffeta gown . . . Kati laughing incredulously, provocatively, shouting at me from the far side of the hall, "You're not intending to lock me up, Tibor, are you?"

At times sleep overpowers me without the intervention of those beloved enemies of mine, and I realize to my astonishment that Jansen and Jenny have already returned from their walk. If not, I cross the arterial balcony to the semicircular room with the cupola. I silently push open the half-closed door. I sit down on the wrought-iron bed. Night begins to thin before my eyes. Kati's body emerges from the dark like a phantom. With every passing day more recognizable, familiar, anticipated like a refrain. Her long arm clamped tightly around one of her hunched shoulders, her face hidden by her hair, one knee pulled up to her stomach and the other stretched out, her foot peeking out from under the covers. Her breath like a large swing that flies up into the air, rattling at times as if it wanted to tear itself free from its taut rope. Her talking in her sleep, more like moaning, almost always in that unknown tongue of which I do not understand a single word. Each time I prick up my ears. Each time I try to grasp the unknown sounds. My sweet Slovenian girl, I say to her weakly.

35

I had not intended to lock her up. Had she not thrown those red shoes of hers at me, one landing on my thigh, the other on the larch-wood armoire by the door, and had she not laughed at me so obstinately all the while, and not asked me so provocatively if, by any chance, I was intending to keep her locked in, I probably would not have done it. I would have tried to reason with her, or to find some other way of stopping her from going out. I would have argued that her temperature had been so high that at times I had truly feared for her. When she had fallen asleep lying on me, for example, or when I had bathed her in the tepid water. That such a high temperature could very well have unexpected after-effects. I would have even called Eli Benjamin and asked him to order a few days of recuperation at home for her. Staying in bed, or at least taking siestas, light food, vitamin C . . . I would have suggested some new games, I would have told her new stories, we would have read together, had a nice little dinner. But Kati glared at me as at an opponent who, come what may, she had to defeat – as if she were intent on climbing a high wall beyond which lay the open road and Simon Osterman.

I went up to her.

"Fine – if this is what you want," I said with apparent calm, though I felt the blood rising to my head. I practically stepped over her, opened the kitchen door, and slammed it shut behind me. That little snot-nose! That little snot-nose! What a damn snot-nose she is, I kept saying over and over as I made myself some coffee. I haven't even had any coffee yet, I mumbled, and thought of Ema. By this time in the morning Ema would already have been making me my second cup of coffee. She would knock on the door of my study. Marie-Hélène would lean her chin on her hand. Ema would walk silently up to the desk and place the coffee pot along with two cups on the right-hand corner. She would nod her head barely perceptibly, and look at me for an instant with her boundless eyes: your coffee is still hot, freshly ground – for supper there's some cold meat in the fridge, cheese, bread – don't forget your pills – I wish you a good day, Monsieur Tibor.

My coffee is not as good as Ema's. I suppose it is because Kati buys it at some supermarket, the way she buys everything else, not that she ever does really shop.

That little snot-nose, I mumbled again. Where had she come from? And what is she doing now, sitting there in the middle of the hall? Barefoot, in her flowery dress, ready to . . .

I went over to the door and listened. Nothing . . . Silence, as if she was no longer there.

I poured myself some coffee. I had to do something. About her, of course. To try and figure out where it was that I had veered from my path and how I was going to get back onto it. I had to call Simon: you and I haven't seen each other in quite a while. Yes, well, I'm not counting Picardy or that afternoon in April at the town hall. What I mean is, we haven't seen each other the way we used to. As in having a quick lunch together between your rehearsals, sometimes not even sitting down, oysters, rye bread, sausages, and white wine, and then going for a walk down our little street, from the restaurant to the theatre – So, how are you, Tibor? Well enough. And what about you, Simon? I'm fine. Can't complain. Anyway, I see nothing's changed. What do you mean? Leopards, martens, squirrels, badgers, you and me. You and me.

Of course I am going to call Simon. I will call him today. Walk down our street with him, those three hundred metres of sincerity between us. A narrow, winding, musty, shadowy, forgotten street. Simon, I want to talk to you about Kati. Please leave her alone, she is not a woman for you – after all, she is mine . . . yes, mine, I don't know how else to put it . . . let's forget what happened in Picardy, things like that do happen, but promise me that you will not lay another finger on her, and not only a finger . . . Simon, promise me. Yes, that's all I have to say. Promise me.

36

Our house arrest, which lasted two long days, turned into a skirmish, a duel, a battle for the upper hand. In those two days we each deployed all our tactics, strategy, and weapons: on Kati's side resolve, doggedness, cunning, a flair for lightning-fast reaction and quick assessment of situations, but also futile stubbornness and an inexplicable susceptibility to things irrelevant. I too had resolve, rather less doggedness, a flair for reaction and gauging situations, but also a definite sense of humour, not to mention the absurd, which can be of great help in a crisis.

During those two days we each marked out our territory, from a distance eyeing each other's demarcation lines, or the extreme limit to which the other was prepared to go.

And during those two days, from the first morning incident to the evening of the following day, we felt far more like a couple than we ever had during our times of peace, or rather our moments of warmth towards one another, closeness, togetherness, joy, and even love. Perhaps not a couple like Monsieur and Madame Jansen, or the young couples that walk down the Champs-Elysées on Saturday afternoons. But still a couple.

During these two long days of high tension, the first part of which Kati spent in the hall, the second in the bathroom, she put on her high-heeled shoes and strutted up and down the hall while I sat at my desk. Or she bathed, made herself up, combed her hair, and sprayed herself with perfume, as if she was about to go out. Two days, during which she ate absolutely nothing and, one could say, grew thinner before my very eyes. Two days, during which she acted as if she were avoiding me, and yet did everything she could to grab my attention and get on my nerves. Two days, during which, though unpremeditatedly, I tore her dress with the red tulips she had worn to our restaurant near the boulevard Saint-Germain. Two days, during which we yelled at each other things we did not even think. She, for instance: that I am an old fool with a febrile imagination who would do better to employ it elsewhere. I: that she was obviously prepared to throw herself into the arms of any man who crossed her path.

She: that she was amazed I could be so jealous in such a cheap way. I: that she was ill-mannered, that evidently no one had ever boxed her ears, and that one had to wonder what her father had been up to all those years, yes, her father . . . After two days of endless tension and extreme exhaustion, after that final phrase which, like all the others, I had shouted in the bathroom in a storm of rage and frustration as the water poured from shower behind us, Kati suddenly turned to me, grabbed me by the wrist, and said, "Let's put an end to this, Tibor. Right away, right now."

The sleeve of her black flowery dress was ripped along the seam, decapitating a long tulip and uncovering a part of her shoulder. Her face was grave, almost frightened, and the grip of her hand on my wrist became tighter. Was it her uncovered shoulder, the expression on her face, exhaustion, or something else? I really do not know, but what I did was to push her suddenly and without warning under the streaming shower and get in after her. She gasped in astonishment.

After those two endless days of war, Kati and I stood together beneath the streaming water in my bathroom. The warm water doused us like a liberating downpour. In an instant we were drenched . . . Kati's hair and face, her uncovered shoulder . . . The tulips on her dress crumpled, recoiling timidly from the sudden deluge . . . My shirt, my trousers . . . my socks, sodden in the rising pool beneath our feet . . . I caressed her hair, wiped the water from her face . . . After those two torturing days of war, it was I who was laughing . . . I caressed her eyes and her forehead, and laughed and laughed . . . while she remained impenetrably grave, as before . . . for an instant I even thought that she was crying, that the drops trickling down her cheeks were warmer and denser than the water streaming over us . . . for an instant I thought she was crying . . .

37

I reached out and turned off the tap behind Kati. Our rain ceased in an instant, while the water kept trickling off us. Once more I dried her hair, her face, her neck. My hand, as if involuntarily, slipped down to her bare shoulder.

"Tomorrow we shall go and buy a new dress. Just like this one, OK?"

She shook her head.

"Why not?" I asked in surprise.

"Because I bought it at the department store in Lille," she said finally.

"In Lille? That's fine – so we'll go to Lille," I said, kissing her bare shoulder. "Lille, Lille . . ." I mumbled, continuing to kiss her shoulder. "But what in God's name were you doing in Lille?"

She did not answer, but nestled up to me.

My God! Lille became a magic word for me – my "Open Sesame!" I felt her two small sheep, now no longer timorous, but rising powerfully beneath the wet cloth. I felt her stomach, just as strong and flat, pressing against mine. I felt her thighs, and the waters rising in them, two channels with only one source.

Kati's breathing grew heavy.

I turned and lit a star-shaped Moroccan brass lamp with

countless little holes through which the light poured as through a sieve. When I turned back and looked at Kati, she stood before me, the most beautiful being I had ever set eyes on, tinted by a mesh of light, her wet dress clinging to her like a second skin, and above all else, that bare shoulder. I came so close to her that I felt her breath on my neck and chest, grabbed her wet sleeve and, with a single sweep, ripped it in two. Kati laughed out loud and began unbuttoning my shirt. I helped her so it would happen faster. I reached my hand between her legs where she was warm, sticky and wet. I started pushing upwards, her inner thigh against my wrist, until she began to moan. I lifted her upwards, pushing her against the wall, pressing her into me, no, it was she who was pressing me into her, me, her, me, her . . . I whispered into her ear, foolish things, obscenities, Lille, what were you up to in Lille, Kati, Katarina, my love . . . we became increasingly feverish, our stomachs slid against each other as they had done that night during Kati's fever . . . The expression on her face became increasingly empty . . . Moans, ever more deep and gurgling, rose from her throat . . . she became heavier, wider, with every second releasing herself more to my hands . . . until she called out as the birds do in Picardy . . . an inhuman call. I too called out, right after her.

She remained pressed against me for a while, resting in my arms.

"O Tibor," she whispered in my ear. She wanted to add something, but evidently thought better of it and laid her head on my shoulder.

I pulled her away from the wall and lowered her to the floor. Our legs were trembling.

Only now did we really look at each other. Only now did I notice that she was smaller than she had seemed in the past. Barefoot, she barely reached my chin. I moved closer. Yes, she came exactly up to my chin. Somehow I have always been touched by women's difference in height, how they grow shorter when they step out of their high heels. I embraced her and raised her off the floor until we were eye to eye.

"My little girl," I said.

Kati burst out laughing again, but this time joyfully, effervescently, and I thought of our flower bobbing away down the Seine.

"Let go of me," she whispered.

"Oh no I won't," I whispered back, pressing her closer to me.

"Let go of me, Tibor . . . Let go . . . Can't you see I can't breathe?"

"So what. As long as I am with you."

Finally I lowered her back to the floor, and she breathed out.

"You're completely crazy," she whispered, bending down, picking up our wet clothes, and putting them on top of the washing machine.

"Tomorrow we're off to Lille," I said.

38

The following day autumn began. I sat at my desk and gazed at it through the window. My piece of sky was a monochrome blue. The light had become more intense and thick in the last few days. The few trees below me were beginning to lose their leaves. Now and then a leaf would even float past my window, as if it had lost its way in the wind, or lost its trifling sense of gravity. Each changing of the seasons has always awakened in me a feeling of unease. How many new autumns and winters had I awaited? How many hopes and expectations had I placed in these bends in time? As if I might be able to squeeze out of them something new, something intense. As if with every passing year time became thicker.

Farkas called me around ten. How are you? Why don't you ever call? And your little doe? How's your little doe? Are you working? Yes, that's exactly what I mean: are you working? You know my opinion. It's been quite a few years now since you've written anything, you son of a lion. Nothing. That's what I said – nothing. A little article for a newspaper here and there, an interview . . . nothing worth mentioning. Nowadays every Tom, Dick, and Harry is writing for the newspapers. It's true that *The New New Héloïse* did well enough in its own way, I'm not saying it didn't . . . but *Agathe's Smile* didn't really sell. Too complex, as I told you right from the start. Do you remember what you said a few years back? Yes, a few years back, I don't exactly remember when. A romance novel, you said, needs two characters, a man and a woman, along with a few silhouettes in the background. All fine and simple: a man and a woman . . . A book which one picks up and doesn't put down again until one gets to the very last word on the very last page. Do you remember, you son of a lion?

No, I do not remember, I thought as I placed the receiver back on the hook and began once more to look through the papers in front of me. I truly do not remember. A man and a woman. Not really that important, after all. What is important is the new autumn, and the fact that Kati and I are going to Lille.

I looked at the last words on the previous page. "Tomorrow we're off to Lille."

Lille! I don't believe it! Though I really did utter those words. The whole beginning of the dialogue is real. I really did turn off the tap behind her, and the water stopped streaming on us. I really did dry her hair and face. I also touched her bare shoulder, which drew me like a magnet. Her skin as always was relentlessly smooth. I suggested that we should go and buy a new dress the following day. And she really had shaken her head and told me she had bought it in Lille. "Let's go to Lille," I had said. All that is true. And that star-shaped brass lamp which I had bought in Morocco, its light particularly tender, really does hang in the bathroom. But that is all.

All the rest is not true. All the rest I invented, and I put my sultry invention to paper. Chapter thirty-seven. The love scene in the bathroom. The only real love scene in the whole novel. Daring and fiery, even though it took place beneath a stream of tepid water. A scene that ended like a new beginning. "My little girl . . . Tomorrow we're off to Lille."

In reality, "Lille" was not our magic word, our almighty Sesame, or a new beginning. Kati had stepped out of the shower, grabbed the nearest towel, and wrapped herself in it.

"Good night," she had said, and walked out of the bathroom. Good night. Good night.

It was that night, as Kati lay asleep on her wrought-iron bed and I sat writing chapter thirty-seven that finally, after all that time, I realised that we would never love one another. That we would never love one another the way we had in that short thirty-seventh chapter. Perhaps differently, definitely differently. How was it possible that I had not realized this earlier? Definitely not in the way that the man and the woman beneath the liberating downpour had, I said to myself, and decided that I would keep chapter thirty-seven as a memento, a relic of an act of love that never took place.

39

"Hello, Simon. I thought I might find you home at this hour . . . Well, anyway, let's meet as usual – one o'clock in the rue Fougères. Call me back if you can't make it."

I left the message on his answering machine. In the morning his phone had rung unanswered, and later on his machine was on. I also called his agent, who assured me that he was in Paris: Next week he is leaving for a short tour in Israel. After Israel he will be conducting in Paris. I hope you will attend, Monsieur Tibor.

I set out around midday. Kati had already left. There was a note for me on the kitchen table: "I'm not here. I'll be back this evening. When shall we go out together?"

I walked down the boulevard Haussmann. It was only when I was halfway there that I realized I was walking too fast, that I was out of breath, that I was obviously in a hurry – that I wanted to settle things with Simon as soon as possible. I was going to have a talk with him as we walked down our street together. I would tell him everything. In a few words, concisely. That Kati was not for him. That I knew her well, and that I was getting to know her better every day. That she was sensitive – much more so than one would think. Vulnerable, surprisingly vulnerable. I do not know what took place between the two of you in Picardy, nor do I want to. All I know is that she fell ill the following day. I do not want her to fall ill again, nor do I want anything else to happen to her. Do you understand? That's all I have to say.

I waited for him until two. The place opposite me at my table remained empty, though otherwise the restaurant was packed.

"I am waiting for somebody," I kept telling people who wanted to sit there or take the chair away. At two Monsieur Jacques, the owner, suggested that perhaps he should serve me lunch anyway.

"I don't think he is going to come," he said.

This is the first time since the long evening and the even longer night during which Simon and I had crossed swords over Brahms and during which that reserved friendship of ours had begun, I said to myself as I walked home, this is the first time that Simon has stood me up. Of course, there have been times when we cancelled our meeting at the very last moment. But neither of us has ever let the other just sit there, drumming his fingers on the table and staring at the door, at unknown faces and an empty chair.

Perhaps I had called him too late. Perhaps at dawn this morning Kati had slipped between his sheets. Needless to say, it all fitted: when I got up, she had already left. And that would be why Simon hadn't picked up the phone. I myself would hardly have picked up the phone had I been in bed with a woman like Kati. And when I left a message later on, they were perhaps having breakfast at his glass table by the window, not far from the phone. When they heard my voice they quickly looked at one another. And who knows where they are now. Simon can easily take off a day or two before his Israel tour. A day or two with Kati-Katarina-Grushenka. Who knows what he calls her . . . Kati? Katarina? Or Grushenka?

I felt feverish, and my ears began to buzz so that I couldn't even hear the traffic around me and had to stop. I leaned against a tree on the boulevard. The buzzing became louder and louder, as if an invisible swarm of bees were whirling about my head. I closed my eyes and began to breathe deeply. Sweat trickled down my back. I held onto the tree. Slowly, very slowly, the bees began to move away until they disappeared completely. For a while I remained slumped against the thick trunk.

"Is something wrong, Monsieur?" I heard a child's voice ask. A boy with a plaster cast on his arm and a school bag over his shoulder was staring at me curiously.

"Yes, something is wrong," I said, and thought again of Kati and Simon.

When I got home, I lay down on the sofa in the kitchen. Kati had really turned my life upside down. Who would have believed that one day I would take my afternoon nap in the kitchen, particularly on that valuable, stylish piece of furniture Baleli had bought at God knows what auction, and which now keeps company with dishes, wooden spoons, pots and pans, and other kitchen utensils?

I fell into a deep sleep, and was woken by the clink of a key in the lock and footsteps in the hall. I looked out of the window: day was descending into evening, and the colours of the sky above the neighbouring rooftop had begun to change.

Kati came noisily into the kitchen and stopped in front of me.

"So what do you think, darling?"

I stared at her in silence for a few seconds.

"What made you do a thing like that?" I asked in despair.

"First you must answer my question," she said, and twirled around in front of the sofa. I stared at her. Before me stood a new Kati: bald, ravaged. She had shorn off her hair! The hair I had caressed, the hair I had brushed out of her eyes, the hair that my hand had become entangled in that first evening at Farkas's, the hair I had washed in the bath during the night of her fever. That bright, silky hair that hung in ringlets by her temples. My hair! She had cut it short, almost like a boy's, revealing her slightly protruding ears and narrow neck. Some hair still hung over her forehead, almost hiding the scar above her right eyebrow.

"I prefer you with long hair," I said finally.

"I know," she answered with a pleased look, and patted my arm.

40

Had the matter with Simon not remained so utterly unresolved, had the incident with the oranges not taken place, and had the owner of the Seven Wonders Café not paid me an unexpected visit, the beginning of autumn would have been calm, happy, and filled with work.

Kati mainly stayed at home, "seeing to our needs", as she put it. For the first time since Ema's departure, we actually cleaned the flat. Kati put on her shorts and one of my old shirts, rolled up her sleeves, took a large plastic bag and began cleaning. As I realized too late, cleaning in Kati's eyes meant throwing away all the useless things that accumulate in our lives. And as she and I did not share the same view as to what was useless and what was not, she threw away old newspapers, empty cigarette packs, torn socks and wilted flowers, but also the August telephone bill, the first page of one of my articles (later I was glad it had ended up in the rubbish), and quite a few things from my "previous" life. All this I only discovered some time after our big cleaning day. Whenever I could not find something after that memorable Friday, I would shrug my shoulders and think of Kati's cleaning frenzy. There were times when I felt that she had deliberately thrown away certain objects that had a particular sentimental value for me. It was only later, when I began to understand her revisionist approach to the past, that I was able to see with fresh eyes the day of cleaning that had so selectively ransacked my flat in the Street of the Lily of the Valley.

But, as I have already mentioned, it was one of our most pleasant days together. Kati opened all the windows and doors. Fresh air swept through the flat and the sun shone directly upon us. As the flat grew colder, we put on warmer clothes and continued cleaning with the windows open. Kati sang old Neapolitan songs, as she always did when she thought I was out of earshot. I sat at the piano and tried to accompany her: *"Dove il mare luccica e tira forte il vento . . . su una vecchia terrazza . . . un uomo abbraccia una ragazza . . . dopo che aveva pianto . . . si schiarisce la voce e ricomincia il canto . . . Te voglio bene assai . . . ma tanto tanto bene."*

She fell silent. I turned and saw that she was listening to

me, leaning against the armoire in the hallway.

At midday we ate on the parquet floor in the sun. Kati spread out a white tablecloth and brought the food. As we ate, she put on her new glasses and read aloud a few pages from the book that I had been leafing through on the afternoon when I had realized that she couldn't see well. I wanted to explain something to her about adjectives. The rule is: one adjective, three, or none. The author of that book, on the other hand, systematically used two adjectives before every noun. But I thought better of it, preferring to gaze at her and listen. She sat cross-legged, leaning back against one of the piano legs. She caressed her thigh as she read, now and then glancing at me from behind her glasses. They did in actual fact suit her, making her look like a wayward student. I was getting used to her short hair. Towards the end of our meal on the parquet I could not refrain from asking her what Simon thought of her new haircut. Kati, who usually had a knack for quick answers, simply emitted a small laugh and laid her head on my lap. I think it was the first time she had laid her head on my lap of her own accord and for no particular reason. I closed my eyes and ran my fingers over her face as if I were blind and wanted to memorize her features forever.

"Back to work now, lazybones!" she said, extricating herself and shaking me out of my pleasant drowsiness.

Late in the afternoon, when we finally had a chance to catch our breath, Kati decided to go shopping.

I, on the other hand, settled down in the lily-patterned armchair and gazed up at my piece of sky. My room smelled fresh. The windows had just been washed and the glass gently refracted the light. Books were piled up one on top of the other, papers also. My fountain pen was in its place. The ash-tray too. The wastepaper basket was empty.

I lit a cigarette. My hands reeked of some household cleaner. What sudden peace! A pleasant void. I did not even want to listen to music. Nothing. I just wanted to sit and wait for Kati to return laden with shopping. Old age, perhaps?

At that moment the doorbell rang. At first I thought it was the telephone. Kati had her keys with her. I went to the door. I opened it and before me stood a stout fellow with black hair, thin sideburns, and bloated fingers in which he held a piece of paper. He was out of breath and eyed me carefully, as if it was he who had just opened the door and not I.

"Does a Mademoiselle Gru . . . Grush . . . ejka live here?" he said with difficulty.

"Yes," I answered quickly, as I did not like the way he was mangling her name. He nodded with a sigh of relief.

"She owes me exactly four hundred and fifty francs. And that's not counting the broken glasses."

"Broken glasses?" I echoed.

"Oh, I'm sorry, I haven't introduced myself. I am the owner of the Seven Wonders Café at number 3, rue Jules Verne."

"Seven Wonders?" I asked, taken aback. I had never heard of the rue Jules Verne, but I found the fellow extremely distasteful, and wanted to rid myself of him as soon as possible. I slipped my hand into my pocket.

"First she calls out 'Drinks all round!' and then, when it's time to pay, she's nowhere to be found."

"Nowhere to be found . . ." I echoed. I turned around and walked over to my desk. I took a five-hundred franc note out of a drawer and waved it under his nose.

"You said four hundred and fifty. So let's make it five hundred even, to cover the glasses."

He wiped his forehead with a handkerchief, and then stuffed the banknote and the handkerchief into the same pocket.

"Tell your daughter . . ." he began, almost confidingly.

"Daughter . . ." I echoed again, clasping the word tight in my mouth as if it were completely foreign to me. A silence followed. The fellow shuffled from one foot to the other and eyed me sympathetically.

"I will, I will," I said absently, and closed the door on him.

"Children will be children," I heard him muttering as he began to descend the stairs.

41

After the visit of the man from the Seven Wonders I began spying on her. Yes, spying – opening her mail, rifling through her room, listening in on her telephone calls and, to an extent, listening in on her dreams. Not methodically, nor, for that matter, with particular success. And yet.

I, yes I, R. A. Tibor, as Baleli would say, who have always been a believer in an individual's right to secrecy, in the sum of our singular secrets, in personal space. I, who have held this right to secrecy sacred and valued it more than anything in the world. I, who have always been convinced that only secrecy can make a man and a woman into a true couple. I, who had left Baleli for precisely that reason: because she was obviously more devoted to me than I was to her, and because she expected the same kind of devotion from me, which in her eyes meant first and foremost a total lack of secrecy between the two of us. And it must be remembered that I had come to an unwritten agreement with Kati, of which in a sense I had been proud. Kati-Katarina-Grushenka, I told myself, is after all the perfect woman for me. A woman who penned only one clause into her marriage contract: "But we won't ask each other any questions." A woman, a young woman, so young that she could easily be my daughter, who regards our relationship as completely uncommitted, or rather autonomous and fully dedicated to the here and now. No past or future. I don't love you for what you used to be, what you would have wanted to be, or what you perhaps will be. I love you because you are you and I am I. And that's all there is to it.

A contract, an idea, which I had respected and, in a sense, was perfectly happy to adhere to. Had I asked her what had taken place that night in Picardy when she and Simon had gone out onto the beach? Had I not been as silent as the grave throughout the whole trip back from Paris, not saying a word until after Eli Benjamin had gone? Did I wake up the head with its coarse black hair that was lying next to hers, did I drag him out of the bed? Did I grab her wrist and force her to sit down again that night in the Italian restaurant when she got up in the middle of our dinner, telling me that she had a rendezvous? No. I had simply looked on weakly as she moved away between the tables. I had even noticed some men's eyes following her.

After the visit of the rue Jules Verne fellow, I turned into what I did not want to be. After the visit of the rue Jules Verne fellow I punctured one of the last balloons of my purity and self-esteem, mixed with pride and above all arrogance.

Kati came back with oranges, or, to be more precise, behind

a pile of oranges. When I heard her key turn in the lock, I got up and went to meet her. The moment I opened the door of my study and entered the hall, I heard her cry out, and a wild avalanche of tumbling oranges poured over the floor.

"Good evening, my dear oranges! Please step in, my dear oranges! This way, my dear oranges! Why don't you make yourself at home!" she shouted, waving two large empty bags in the air, while the oranges tumbled over one another, colliding against the walls and the bathroom door.

"I want a word with you, Kati," I said to her from the doorway of my study, as if nothing had happened, as if I had not noticed the oranges.

"With me? Right now when the mademoiselles oranges have dropped in?" she called out from the other end of the hall, her face and eyes shining. "Please make yourselves comfortable, my sweet oranges."

"Now!" I added.

"Tibor! Think of the long journey they have behind them – Israel, Israel–Paris. Not to mention their trip with me down the rue Balzac and up five flights of stairs. Luckily I ran into Monsieur Jansen," she said, continuing her game, trying to stay completely serious, even though her mouth kept breaking into a smile. She seemed elated and excited. Drops of sweat glistened on her brow.

"Kati!" I said in an admonishing tone.

She sat down on the floor, leaned against the door, sighed deeply, and looked with obvious delight at all the oranges lying around.

"Is something the matter?" she asked, without looking at me.

"How about telling me what happened in the rue Jules

Verne?" I replied, somewhat less patient, and took a step towards her.

"Jules Verne?" she asked, as if it was the first time she had heard the name.

"The Seven Wonders in the rue Jules Verne," I added.

"The rue Jules Verne and the . . ."

She burst out laughing, snatched up three oranges, and began juggling them.

I went over to her, crouched down, and snatched the oranges out of the air. I felt my lips tremble with fury.

"The Seven Wonders!" I repeated emphatically. "The Seven Wonders Café, and that stout fellow with the sideburns! Drinks for everyone! Breaking glasses!"

She looked at me as if she truly had no idea what I was talking about. Then she suddenly got up and walked past me into my study. I sat on the floor for a few moments, looking at the hall filled with oranges, then followed her.

I stopped in the doorway. She was standing in front of the bookshelf and seemed to be looking for something. I kicked at an orange that had rolled between my feet.

"Calm down, calm down! Look at me, am I aggravated?" she murmured, picking up the orange.

She found my old street guide of Paris with its faded cover and, without turning, threw it at me across the room.

"Catch!" she called out. "And take a good look through it. Look under J. J, as in Jean or Jacques, and tell me if you find anything. Rue Jules Verne." And then she suddenly added in a conciliatory tone: "While you're looking, I'll go to the kitchen and squeeze some oranges for you."

42

The rue Jules Verne remained an unexplained matter between the two of us. It is true that even I, who took pride in being an adopted Parisian, which means knowing the city better than the Parisians themselves, had never heard of the rue Jules Verne, nor of the Seven Wonders Café, and nor did I have any intention of looking them up in any Parisian map or street guide. But the fact remained that I had not dreamt up the stout fellow with the sideburns, or that I had given him a five-hundred franc bill. And it was also true that, all things considered, I was partly to blame for Kati's idleness and wasting of time. Was it not I who had offered her a life of leisure at my side? Had I not explained to her that the pressure of having to earn one's daily bread subjugates the body and the soul, that it hinders thought, but that it is up to us to look all around ourselves, to find our blind alleys, and even at times to be prepared to experience boredom? Oh, boredom is nothing but the unfurling of time, I had said to her.

And in some things my Kati took me completely at my word, was even obedient.

And while I began to move away from my ideas, at least from some of them, gradually beginning to detest them, Kati began adopting them and implementing them right before my very eyes. Live this town to the fullest, its streets, the ones you know and the ones you do not know, its wide avenues and the boulevards with shady trees! Its intense sky and the long farewell of the days! All the marvellously unknown faces! Her eyes would whisper of all that pent-up loneliness and alienation when she came home. While I listened for her to slip her key into the lock and for her footsteps in the hall, and waited for the door of my study to open so that I would see her before me.

A few days ago Farkas, with his usual feverishness, invited me to one of his cocktail parties. Before he had a chance to say another word, or to develop one of his theories, I told him that I saw no reason on God's earth, no reason whatsoever, to dress, put on a pair of shoes, comb my hair, order a taxi, and make my way through his courtyard with its pseudo-Greek columns and up to the second floor, to hand over my coat, and to immerse myself in his crowd of pseudo-artists and pseudo-intellectuals.

"Is something wrong, son of a lion?" he asked.

"Oh, no, no . . . everything is fine. It's just that there is only one face I want to see, one person I want to be with, and as this person is about to come back any moment now, I have no intention of stirring out of the house."

"The doe?" he asked in a worried tone.

I laughed in answer.

"Be careful, son of a lion," he muttered, and hung up.

43

We had fallen into the habit of talking after dinner. This habit had taken root a few nights before, like a hardy plant. Kati would quickly make dinner. Cooking was not one of her strengths, though she did know how to surprise me with unusual and not always successful combinations. Her beetroot salad, for instance, with pale-yellow potatoes and pale-green grapes, was definitely more inspired by harmony of colour than of taste. After dinner she would roll up her sleeves and say, "Shall we?"

"Shall we" meant going to the room with the piano, where Kati had set up our new salon on the Anatolian carpet and velvet cushions, near a bouquet of flowers, beneath the crystal chandelier, between the piano and the wall. We would take a bottle of red wine, cigarettes and paper. Kati made herself comfortable among the pillows, rolled onto her stomach, rested her chin on her palms, and silently watched me open the bottle, fill the glasses, light the cigarette, lean back against the wall, and suck in my first mouthful of smoke. Then she would come and sit in front of me, take a piece of paper, and begin folding it with her nimble fingers.

"Where were we?" she would ask each time.

I would suck in my second mouthful. Nowhere, is what I wanted to answer. Nowhere and everywhere. Our conversations were fantastically disconnected, without a thread. We flitted from one topic to another with the utmost ease and without prejudging their logic or coherence, without striving to find conclusions, syntheses, or even antitheses. The silences, smiles, the clinking of glasses, my caresses (Kati's new hairstyle, her short shock of hair, her narrow neck seemed made for my hand) punctuated our phrases, mostly with ellipses, and at times with question marks or exclamation marks. We carefully steered clear of certain topics – I avoided any mention of Simon or her nocturnal moans in what I imagined must be Slovene, and she too avoided certain subjects. But otherwise any and every topic was grist for our mill. Time and destiny, can one take them in hand, redirect their course? – Kati would ask – Is that which is not and never was invariably more valuable than that which is? Can one purge oneself of the past, can one correct it? Yes, correct it, is what she said.

I have always loved talking to women. Kitty-cat Silvia, for instance, and our frank discussions about eroticism over cream cakes – between sessions with her trying on elegant gowns that she never bought, but which she modelled with delight, admiring herself at great length in the mirror – and the silken ruthlessness with which she could force me to confront myself. And had I been more sharp-sighted during those evenings before Simon's return from Israel, had I listened with a more attentive ear to Kati's voice, to the subdued tone and the quavering uncertainty, and had I noticed the unusual dance of her hands, I would have seen that our evening conversations were not as fantastically disconnected as I had thought. Perhaps I would have sensed that like Silvia she was pushing me imperceptibly but persistently in the same direction, that she was patiently handing me the thread with which I could have easily bound our hearts together or rather unbound hers. Or is this also perhaps just an impression, one of those impressions that grab us when it is already too late, and we begin to understand things that are irrevocably behind us?

44

Simon returned the following week. I did not need to call him or his agent to assure myself of his return. Overnight, Kati became irritable, prickly, distracted, and pensive. She barely touched her breakfast. She locked herself in the bathroom. She began pacing the flat like a lion in a cage. At least three times she put on her shoes and then took them off again, and God knows how often she changed clothes.

I sat at my desk and tried to keep my cool.

"Tibor, Tibor," she called out, bursting into my study and hurrying up to me. "Do you remember how you said that we should go and buy a new dress?"

So all of a sudden she was in a hurry. Yesterday and the day before, and all those days that she had spent with me, she had not needed a new dress. And now today, like lightning striking out of a clear blue sky, she needed one, and what a hurry she was in!

"Tibor, don't you remember?" she asked, nestling up to me and sitting on my lap.

I liked it when she sat on my lap like that and laid her head on my shoulder – I had the impression I could hear her thoughts cavorting around her head. I liked feeling her weight on my thighs. She has fully recovered from her illness, I thought. Yes, she has gained weight. She is just as she was before. Except for her hair, which is slowly beginning to grow again over her forehead, the top of her head, and her narrow neck.

"Tibor, don't you remember?" she repeated impatiently.

I looked towards the window. On top of everything else, a drizzling rain had begun to fall. In the last few days autumn had taken over. The weather was getting colder, and a light, nagging wind had begun to howl. No, I didn't want to go out today, even though I have often wanted to shop for dresses with her. I wanted to choose all her clothes. All of them: warm pullovers, a winter coat, trousers, a long dress, even her underwear, even her panties. I had already looked at various display windows and written down a few addresses.

"Say that we'll go," she whispered, as if she too could hear my thoughts.

But the day had begun badly, and our afternoon of shopping did not unfold according to my plans. Never before had Kati been so capricious or so obstinate. She huddled under my umbrella and stared glumly in front of her. Whenever we entered a shop, she would look around disappointed, shrug her shoulders, grimace, and ask inappropriate questions that made me feel increasingly uncomfortable. It was obvious that she did not know what she wanted, even though she assured me that that was not the case. She wanted a new dress, she said. Not a coat, not warm pullovers, not a long tweed skirt, not trousers. A dress, she insisted, looking me coldly in the eye. Only one. A beautiful one, a very beautiful one. She knew what kind of dress she wanted. If she saw it, she would know it was the one she was looking for, she said, and then added, "What's wrong with you today, Tibor?"

With me? I looked at her in amazement, but chose to say nothing. Was I the one who was losing my senses because Simon Osterman was back in Paris? Was I the one who was staring glumly straight ahead, dreaming about him? Was I the one who didn't know what he wanted? How many shops had we already been in? Fifteen? Twenty?

On top of everything we began feeling chilly. At least I did. Kati disappeared into one of the shops, and I felt the damp cold begin to seep through me, and my feet began to ache. And mademoiselle had the nerve to ask what was wrong with me! I paced up and down the pavement. I lit a cigarette. If only

I knew which shop she had gone into. I would tell her that I was going to wait for her at the café across the street. Or even at Farkas's. We weren't all that far away from the rue Bonaparte, or from the rue Jacob where Baleli has her antique shop. In the days before Kati-Katarina-Grushenka I would drop in at Baleli's shop at least once a week. She has probably gone to telephone Simon, I suddenly thought. Of course. This morning she had also kept trying to call somebody, hanging up each time without saying a word.

"Tibor! Tibor! Look!" I heard her call from the other side of the street, and I turned towards her voice. I did not see her right away as the street was filled with traffic. It wasn't until a bus rolled forward and a red van drove out of its parking place that I saw her on the other side of the rue de Rennes. The image is irrevocably engraved in my memory. Even today, with our life together definitely a thing of the past, I can still see her standing in that very same place whenever I walk through the lower part of the rue de Rennes. I go and stand where I stood on that cold afternoon, between a shoe shop and a sandwich booth. When the cars finally move, I see her on the pavement, or rather with one foot on the pavement and the other in the street, and she is hopping from one foot to the other. She waves and smiles at me.

"I found it, Tibor! Look! Look!" she shouts, and the passers-by turn and stare.

She is wearing a long dress the colour of burnt grass. Low cut, the cloth at her breasts pleated into a few folds like a decorated balcony, and the rest extremely simple: bare arms, tight belt, very feminine hips, a steep fall and ripple of the cloth to her ankles.

"Wait, wait!" she shouts, and turns around so that I can see her from all angles. "What do you think?" She twirls around once more, and the cloth brushes again over her thighs and calves.

And I just stand there, I stand and look across the rue de Rennes, until the image pales and slowly disappears before my eyes.

45

Her agitation grew day by day. Farewell to those cosy mornings of ours. Farewell to our long afternoons. Farewell our evenings, with their heavy rain of words and the slow rise of alcohol in our blood. The litmus paper of every new morning showed but one colour: nightmare grey. Kati continued to roam through the flat like a captured bird. She clenched her fists, rested her forehead on them, and stood on the balcony staring out in front of her. When the telephone rang, she surged up like the sea before a storm. It was evident that she was expecting something to happen. When she could no longer sit still, she muttered that she was going out for a while.

The instant she crossed the threshold, I got up to follow her. I had learned quite a few tricks in the past few days. How to open a letter imperceptibly. How to follow Kati along a main street. And also along side streets, which was quite a bit more complicated. What to do when she entered a shop, for instance, or a café. And particularly the Métro. The Métro became horror, my black hole. I must confess that in the beginning I was more than clumsy, and that at times I had the impression that Kati was well aware that I was following her, and that she was even gently leading me on. And I was now more convinced than ever that Simon was behind all of this. That she was trying to cover her tracks so she could get in touch with him, which was obviously not a simple matter, as Simon is uncommonly busy – rehearsals, meetings, study, piano. But a man can always make an exception in his schedule and steal an hour or two for an afternoon of love. Who wouldn't?

She led me all the way down the avenue de Friedland. At the corner of the street that cuts across it, she went into a shop that sold musical scores. Three streets further down she bought herself a *pain au chocolat* at a corner bakery, engaging the woman behind the counter in a long conversation. As I stood watching her from behind a bus stop, a dark-skinned young man approached me and invited me to attend a weekly Bible meeting at a nearby Seventh-Day Adventist church. I shook my head quickly. "Aren't you searching for something?" he called after me. Kati said goodbye to the woman behind the counter and set off along the rue Washington. After a lengthy detour down the Champs-Elysées, where I almost lost her a few times, we returned home.

The following day she went to her exercise class. She stopped in front of a wide, two-storeyed building with a brightly lit ground floor. She walked up and down on the pavement for a while, obviously waiting for somebody. When she finally went inside, I walked up to one of the windows and peeked in through a gap in the venetian blind. Yes, she was taking an exercise class. She was doing some more or less rhythmical movements with a group of young people, mainly women, following the instructions of a powerful male voice. I turned towards the voice. In the corner of the exercise room stood a man of medium height with short dark hair . . . with short dark hair and . . . I looked at his left hand – a silver ring.

When she came back, I was waiting for her in my study.

"Where were you?" I asked.

"At the cinema," she answered with the utmost calm, looking me straight in the eye.

Towards evening she took a shower, changed clothes, wrapped my silk scarf around her neck, and walked down the rue Balzac. She disappeared suddenly around the corner by the Palais Rothschild. I went to the triangular *place* in front of the Palais. I looked in the bakery a few steps further down the street, and even in the flower shop. "May I help you, Monsieur?" I leaned against the display window. I felt my throat tightening. I had lost her. And yet, the earth couldn't have simply swallowed her up. I looked around one more time. The flower seller was peering at me anxiously from behind her white and red roses. I continued walking towards the corner of avenue Hoche. Suddenly I heard footsteps. Footsteps coming closer.

"Where are you going, Tibor?" she asked in a cold, even aloof voice.

"What about you?" I replied without looking at her. My voice was a taut string on the point of breaking.

"The Métro. Place des Ternes. Do you want to come with me?"

We walked beside each other and our feet gradually fell into step. We still did not look at one another.

"Where are you going?" I uttered, the string stretching even tauter.

"The Métro."

"And then?"

"And then?"

I felt that I could only utter one phrase at a time. That otherwise something would burst in my throat and that pain would tear through my head. We were nearing the Place des Ternes. The traffic light blinked red in front of us.

"Why don't you just follow me? Go on! The first passageway to the left, the stairs, the second passageway, this time the main one which has an escalator on the other side, and then take the escalator . . . "

"Enough!" I shouted.

I grabbed her by the shoulders, intent on hurting her. It was only now that we looked at each other. Her face was pale and smooth. Only her eyes stared at me defiantly, her lips trembling slightly.

"Enough? You mean you've had . . . "

"Enough!" I groaned again. We were standing in the middle of the *place*, a few steps away from the entrance to the Métro. A few passers-by turned and looked at us.

"You are right. I agree with you. I have also had enough!" she said, freeing herself from my grip. I followed her for a few steps and then stopped.

Kati, I wanted to shout after her. Wait, wait! But my vocal cords remained rigid . . . I didn't mean it! I didn't! Kati! I felt my legs shaking, and knew that I had to sit down. Yes, sit down, sit down immediately.

"Good night, Tibor!" she shouted from the first step of the Métro entrance without turning back, and disappeared before my eyes below ground.

46

Never, since I have lived in the nest above the Périphérique (as Farkas likes to call my flat in the rue Balzac), had I gone so many times in a single day to the Place des Ternes. Never had I crossed so many times the boulevards and avenues cutting through it, and walked up and down it so persistently among the flower sellers. The day was incredibly cold and clear. The flower sellers rubbed their frozen hands together. The flowers and other decorative plants surrounded them like picturesque little gardens. I do not know if I was really expecting her to reappear at the same spot where she had disappeared, at that Métro entrance in the middle of the flowery *place*, or if I simply wanted to be close to it. That first evening, and then the following day, I felt as if the earth had abducted her as it had abducted Proserpina, and that she had disappeared into its maw or into the maw of God knows which Vulcan. And that the earth would vomit her up again, returning her to me as it had taken her away from me.

But finally I gathered my scattered thoughts. Kati had left. Left home, I repeated at the top of my voice, as if I had gone deaf, unable to hear even my own thoughts. So simple. Left home. Left. Gone. Run away. Ha! Proserpina? Vulcan? Simon. Simon Osterman. And Kati-Katarina-Grushenka.

After that first night of torture, and the first day that I spent roaming around the Place des Ternes and my empty flat, I began to gather my exhausted thoughts. Farkas telephoned me, as he always did, at the worst possible moment.

"How are you? It's getting cold, isn't it? No more summer.

What are you doing, you son of a lion? A pity you didn't come to the party! Where's Tibor, everyone was asking. No one's seen hide nor hair of him. What's he up to? And what about the doe? How's the doe doing?"

"I don't know," I answered in complete honesty.

But I will find out, I told myself. I will look for her. Paris is not so big that I can't find her.

I was worn out and exhausted, I felt I was succumbing to a cold, and yet . . . Once I had brought her home, there would be ample time to recuperate. I would sleep, eat, read, sit in the lily-patterned armchair, make tea, and look at the sky. Yes, I will go to Simon. To his second-floor flat. I will ring his doorbell. I will walk into his living room with its view of the Seine and its two pianos . . . "No!" I almost shouted. I did not want to see her in the middle of that large living room with its door to the bedroom . . . I did not want to see her at his place. I could not. I really could not. I would tackle things differently. Yes, differently!

47

"Simon Osterman is in the main auditorium, isn't he?" I asked in the most neutral voice I could muster.

"Simon Osterman is in rehearsal, which means he is not here."

"In the main hall?" I insisted in the same colourless voice.

Standing sentinel by the stage entrance, eyeing me coldly, was a tall woman with a protruding jaw, who, had she been even minimally observant, would have recognized me immediately.

"He is not to be disturbed," she said.

Kati would have been proud of me had she seen me force my way past this long-legged guard, I thought, as I climbed the stairs and made my way along the narrow corridors. In extreme circumstances my imagination leaps into action. In extreme circumstances I can always rely upon it. I opened a side door of the auditorium and made my way through the seats to the last row of the stalls. Simon, with his infallible ear that missed not the tiniest sound, turned his head in my direction. But the lights of the hall were dimmed, and it was impossible to see the last few rows of the stalls from the conductor's podium. Simon continued the rehearsal.

This was the first time I had ever watched and listened to him covertly. "Stop!" he shouted after a few bars, banging his baton on the podium. "Stop! Stop! Start again! From the top!" In his white shirt, with his sleeves rolled up, he looked, as he always did, like a dark bird. He waved and fluttered his arms as if they were wings. His upper body was hunched forwards like that of a bird of prey eyeing its victim far below in the valley. From time to time he stamped his foot helplessly, or shuffled in agitation from one foot to the other. "Stop! Stop!" he shouted again in a shrill voice that tore through the air. He placed his baton on the podium and buried his face in his hands in a pathetic gesture.

I got up abruptly. The seat creaked and loudly clapped shut. Simon swung around threateningly towards the hall. I do not know whether he recognized me from where he stood, but he whispered something to the first violinist, walked across the stage past the orchestra, and furiously made his way down to the stalls. It seems he cannot control his limp when he is exhausted and his nerves are on edge, I thought to myself as he came towards me, or perhaps I have never examined him so coldly before. Yes, with every step he took his left leg dragged behind in a quite strange way. He did not see me until we stood almost face-to-face. Evidently the lights had been shining straight into his eyes.

"Tibor! You, here?" he said in astonishment. He bit his lip and wiped his forehead. His face was sallow, drops of sweat trickled down it, and his shirt was wet beneath his armpits.

"Why didn't you tell me you were here?" he asked in a conciliatory tone.

"Kati, Simon, Kati," I uttered, as if I were reciting a geometric formula.

"Kati?" he asked, lifting his eyebrows in surprise.

"I want her to come back home. Today. I was going to go straight to your house, but then I thought better of it. Listen, Simon, I have to talk to you."

He took me by the elbow and gently led me towards the door.

"No, no," I said, freeing myself from his grip and sitting down on the nearest step.

Simon sighed deeply and sat down next to me. We sat without saying a word, each gathering his thoughts. The musicians folded up their stands and began leaving the stage. The orchestra slowly dispersed. Silence descended on the hall.

"Listen Tibor, I have no idea what you are talking about. Really, I don't. And as you can see, this isn't the best time for us to talk," he said finally, his eyes staring absently in front of him.

"You don't know what I am talking about?" I was almost

shouting, my voice echoing through the empty auditorium.

He looked at me as if seeing me for the first time.

"Tibor, what is wrong with you?"

"With me?"

"Have you looked at yourself in the mirror recently?"

Me? I thought hard. What is wrong with me? And had I looked at myself in a mirror?

Before I could answer, he got up and walked over to a side door. He turned and said simply, "You must excuse me, Tibor."

48

"What is wrong with you?" the talk-show hostess with the platinum-blonde hair also asked me.

She leaned towards me, her long earrings jangling, and I felt her shoulder touch mine. We were sitting next to one another on the cold leather sofa in her living room, with blinds drawn and lights dimmed. We were each holding a second glass of cognac, and we had behind us at least two bottles of Château Margaux '83 – an excellent year, exquisite, according to Fabrice, the owner of a new restaurant on the avenue Carnot.

"What is wrong with me?" I repeated, clumsily taking another swallow. Tulip-shaped cognac glasses always drive me to contortions.

"I shall speak very frankly," she said, turning to me confidingly, her earrings jangling again over her shoulders.

"Please do," I spluttered, my eyes pinned on a swinging earring and the shoulder beneath it.

"I imagined you to be different. How shall I put it? Well, I imagined you as a man who knows how to make choices – friends, acquaintances, women, situations, the programmes he will appear on, the newspapers he writes for, the books he reads . . . A man who definitely knows what he wants . . . who doesn't get mixed up with just anything or anybody . . . People are talking about you . . . A man who isn't even one of their own, if you know what I mean. But I have always looked at you in the best light, from your best side," she dithered, tugging at one of her shoes, which was dangling from her foot.

I stared at the décolleté of her blouse and the taut, pointed breasts beneath. Her legs were crossed, and a triangular opening yawned between her thighs and her short skirt.

"You can imagine how awestruck I was when I first met you. But you are so different today. I know it was you who invited me to dinner, but still . . ."

Her words came to me from far away, even though she was sitting close enough for me to reach out and touch those pointed breasts or feel my way into the tunnel beneath her skirt.

"You seem different . . . more compassionate . . . more gentle – I don't know what you think of this."

I didn't think anything, absolutely nothing. I placed my empty glass on the carpet by our feet and took the opportunity of removing the dangling shoe that was swinging pitilessly from the tips of her toes. Without a pause in the flow of her words she flicked off the other shoe with her bare foot, and it fell onto the table.

"Do you remember the end of our radio show? I got very flustered. I don't know if you noticed. I quoted something from your book, you know, from *Strawberries*. And you just stared at me. Just like you're doing now. There was dead silence. One second, two, three – you lit a cigarette – six, seven, eight . . . I had to muster all my presence of mind, let me tell you, and . . ."

I grabbed her protruding, pear-shaped breasts. First one, then the other. I stretched out my hand to the opening between her skirt and her thighs, which led directly to the entrance of another opening.

"Love is a journey towards a destination we have not chosen . . ." she managed to say.

This line ricocheted through my head as I took off her earrings, her blouse and her skirt, revealing her bronzed skin and her lace undergarments, as my hands fumbled over her hard, muscular thighs, her stomach just as hard and muscular, as I felt my way between her taut breasts and her dark nipples, as I pulled her onto me clumsily, as she straddled me, deftly opening herself to me, as we galloped ahead heaving and crazed, as, panting, she and I reached the edge of darkness, as I was suddenly gripped by a chill, as she, crazed in her saddle, expelled me from her, and I, exhausted, bent over, stalked forward over barren terrain, alone, completely alone, hearing the distant clatter of my horse's hooves.

49

I went to the door three times in a row. I thought I heard mewing outside. Yes, the same raspy whine with which Benz had announced himself when he came back from his afternoon jaunts. Three times in a row I opened the door, and three times

I went down to the fourth floor. Nothing. And definitely not that indomitable black and white beast of mine called Benz . . . Benz – not as in Mercedes Benz, of course, but as in Maria Marguerita Benz.

If someone were to ask me what I did between the day of the deafening, decadent gallop with the platinum-blonde hostess of *As You Like It* and Baleli's visit, I would have replied, "Nothing. I waited. I waited for Kati to come back."

I paced up and down the flat. Never before had my flat struck me as being so large, even when I first moved in and my footsteps had echoed against the empty walls. I counted a hundred and fifty paces walking from the front door, through my study, the room with the piano, the bedroom, the kitchen, and into the semicircular room with the cupola. And an additional fifty if I returned via the arterial balcony. My bedroom, for instance, was definitely not a space put to proper use. I never entered it during the day. And at night I keep wandering from it along the balcony to the semicircular room with the cupola. As it is, the last few nights I have spent on the sofa in the kitchen. God knows what Ema would say if she saw me in the morning, rising from this piece of furniture, whose chiselled frame she had for years waxed and polished to a deep shine.

That afternoon I made a detour over the Place des Ternes to the park in front of the Palais Rothschild. I trod on the fallen leaves, which sank softly beneath my feet. The park was almost empty. A few children with their mothers, a young man wearing a tie holding an open book on his lap, two grey-haired ladies sitting next to each other. I sat down on the bench beneath the tallest plantain tree – the one that reaches above the roof of the Palais and is visible from far away. I folded my arms, crossed my legs, and stared straight in front of me.

What a long autumn day. Nobody hurrying anywhere. The children playing on the grass among the leaves in the hollow. The charm of the park lay precisely in that uneven area between the tall trees. And in the leaves scattered everywhere. A young woman and her child lay in the grass not far from me. The young woman's eyes were closed. Perhaps she was even asleep. The child, not able to walk yet, crawled around her on all fours.

A few months ago, at the beginning of summer, I too had fallen asleep on one of these benches. I do not know how I had imagined back then that I might run into Ema here. Amongst these children, their mothers, and the grey-haired ladies. Ema is definitely not the kind of woman you would find sitting about in a park. It is all so long ago now. When Kati had come home that evening she had sat on my lap. She had just taken a shower, her hair was wet, and her skin still damp. She had pressed herself against me and said, "Now we are alone."

What calm. In the middle of summer Kati and I had roamed about our neighbourhood. The air was still hazy with heat though the day was descending to evening. We entered the Russian church in the rue Daru. We were engulfed by a pleasant coolness, silence, gloom, flickering candles, and the smell of incense. We sat in the stalls under a side-cupola, which, like the main one, was covered in wire mesh as the plaster had begun to crumble. The only sound was the footsteps of an old man lighting fresh candles. I do not remember how long we stayed. I remember Kati leaning over to me and whispering that people had built churches for this silence. A silence they were not able to hear within themselves. A presence they were not able to feel, she had said.

The park was almost empty. The young woman was now really asleep on the grass. Her child, good Lord . . . her child had crawled all the way to the hollow. I got up and went over to the child. For a moment it lifted its head and looked up at me. It had a round, moon-shaped face, black eyes, and a snotty nose with a little yellowish leaf sticking to it. The young woman was still asleep, her face pointing up to the sky.

We were alone now. The child among the leaves, the sleeping mother and I, leaning against the plantain tree. And Kati. During the few seconds in which I debated whether or not I should pick up the child and take it back to its mother, I felt that Kati-Katarina-Grushenka was part of me. As is my right hand, my foot, my shoulder. As the highest branch on the plantain tree is also the plantain. That she was not actually near me, but that in a sense she was. Yes, exactly: she wasn't and yet she was.

Later, Manuel's cockerels came squawking into the park. His cockerels and hens. Manuel was following them with his keys in his hands. I picked up the crawling child and carried it over to its mother. I crouched down next to her and tapped her on the shoulder. Startled, she opened her eyes.

"Oh," she whispered, taking the child and laying it on her chest.

50

When the bell rang the following day and I went to open the door, I felt my hands shake and my heart pound. It was Baleli.

"Oh, it's you," I said, leaning my head towards her cheek.

"Well, one might almost think you were disappointed," she said, turning to me with a smile, her white teeth flashing.

"No, no, I just wasn't expecting you, that's all! Come on in!"

We went through the hall. Her red braid swayed behind her.

"Where are we going?" she asked, stopping in front of the room with the piano.

"The kitchen."

We sat down at the table. I poured her a glass of water. Baleli drinks nothing but water and white wine. I waited for her to comment on the sofa being in the kitchen: such a beautiful piece of furniture, so rare, quite unique, a valuable antique, right in the middle of the kitchen! Has anybody ever seen anything like it!

"You're alone?"

"Yes," I answered, nodding.

"An exercise class?"

"No, no."

"I just happened to be passing, so I thought I'd drop in. I haven't seen you for ages."

I nodded again. It was true, we hadn't seen each other since Picardy.

"A few days ago I was thinking of coming over to your shop," I said.

She picked up her glass and took a few long sips.

"And why didn't you?"

I shrugged my shoulders and lit a cigarette.

"Aren't you smoking too much?" she asked with a worried look.

"No, not really," I answered.

She bent down over her basket and began rummaging around for something. Her braid slid past her shoulders and hung over her eyes. I smelled her perfume, which I would have recognized among a thousand. She was wearing a cobalt-blue dress suit, black stockings, and high heels. Her wedding ring. Thirty years after that auction in the Hôtel Drouot and Baleli is still a beautiful woman, I thought. Her delicate, fair skin is lined with countless fine wrinkles, particularly around the eyes and mouth, the green of her eyes has dimmed, her fingers are swollen . . . but her perfect features have maintained the precise balance of a mathematical equation.

"I brought you something," she said, taking a package wrapped in newspaper out of her basket and placing it in front of me. "I simply had to buy it when I saw it. You know how I am."

"Yes, I do," I said, nodding, and began unwrapping the newspaper.

51

I, too, believed that the body and the soul are inextricably linked. I believed in the soul that lights or obscures the body, and in the body that obscures or lights the soul. That from a certain age we have the kind of face we deserve. And I have always considered myself a discerning observer of faces and bodies, an archivist of their most delicate subtleties. Nothing escapes me, every wrinkle narrates its daily subjection to time, sagging mouths bewail the bitterness they must imbibe, and eyes that have paled show me a horizon that comes closer day by day. Don't look at me like that, Baleli has often said. What are you thinking about, Farkas asks when he catches me staring at him.

Baleli had brought me a tiny vanity mirror, very well preserved, from the late nineteenth century. And when I looked into the mirror, which had instead of a stand a minuscule chest of drawers with two brass handles in the shape of a woman's hands, I suddenly saw it. I saw the new path my face had set out on in a single night. My mouth, the expression around my mouth, I said to myself – has it not lost its furtive hint of scorn?

"Thank you, Baleli," I said with a loud sigh.

I wanted to add something, something like, "Though our marriage was obviously not successful, we can definitely be proud of our divorce!" But I thought better of it, and simply touched her hand, which was lying on the table. She pulled it away, as if I had done something inappropriate.

"I've got to get back to the shop," she said.

"I'll take you there."

Baleli's visit that morning had nothing in common with her usual evening visits, I thought on my way home.

I was going to do some shopping, but changed my mind at the last moment, as if I had had a premonition. I quickened my pace and almost ran home.

"How come you're in such a hurry?" Monsieur Jansen called out after me.

I know it is easy to say all this now that everything is behind us and I am narrating what one could call the final act in Kati's and my story. But anyway, what I remember is hurrying past the concierge, grabbing my mail without the customary – "How are you, Madame Cipriani? Marvellous weather, isn't it?" – seeing the envelope with Simon's handwriting on it, climbing the stairs much faster than usual without stopping on the third floor, and then, panting, coming to a halt at the foot of the last flight of stairs leading up to the fifth floor.

Kati was sitting on the top step. She got up when she saw me. Her cheeks were flushed and her lips chapped, and she was wearing the same masculine outfit she had worn the evening she had disappeared into the Métro. With my silk scarf around her neck and a plastic bag at her feet.

"I forgot my keys," she said, as if we had seen each other only half an hour earlier, and she started coming down the stairs towards me. Halfway down she suddenly threw herself into my arms, so that I almost lost my balance.

"I forgot the keys to the flat," she whispered into my ear, pressing herself against me.

My God, how well I knew her. How my arms had forever learned the measurements of her body. Of that firm torso. Of those shoulders and that swimmer's frame. That waist that I could practically encircle with my hands. The pressure of her pelvic bones that I could feel through her dress. Her taut thighs. And those smooth, curved palms that were holding onto my back.

O how well I knew her.

52

Simon's concert and the reception that followed are the worst moments of Kati's and my story. The beginning of the end, the eclipse of all the heavenly bodies, a tunnel without an emergency exit. And perhaps for Kati the single greatest bravura performance of her whole score. A true black pearl. As for Simon, even today I still am not sure. Simon is one of the greatest conductors of the youngish generation. There is no doubt about that. There is nobody who can stem, curb, dilute, stop the flow of music with the flair and passion that he does. Yes. For stemming, curbing, stopping is in every way a more heroic deed than the powerful unleashing and outpouring of sentiment, which Simon increasingly has his orchestra perform as a hopeless, transitory liberation.

The concert had been scheduled a few days after Kati's return. The envelope with Simon's handwriting contained our invitation. "Simon Osterman cordially invites Tibor and Grushenka . . ." Only the names Tibor, Grushenka, and Simon were written by hand, in a dark-blue ink. The rest of the invitation was printed in gold lettering on a grey background.

Even today I do not know why I accepted the invitation, why I did not turn it down or simply send Kati to the concert alone. Why I did not take her to a restaurant, to the cinema, or for a walk beneath the acacias, especially since in the last few days she had been as soft and sweet as a flower? Why did I not firmly shake my head and announce that we were going to stay at home, that we would lie back on the Turkish carpet, open a bottle of red wine, and talk, yes, talk. Why did I not go home after our first and last unforgettable dance together to the sounds of a harmonica not far from the Place de la Bastille? Why did I not simply take her to the steps of the Opéra, wave goodbye, and go back home? Happiness, however fleeting, is certainly the most effective antidote to reason.

The evening could not have begun on a better note. We dressed for the concert. Kati wore the new silk and velvet dress that was the colour of burnt grass, and I put on my dark-grey suit with a blue shirt and a dark-blue tie. We looked at ourselves in the hall mirror and exchanged a smile. "I like you in that tie," she said. We ordered a taxi. Kati took control of the conversation with the driver while I calmly gazed at the sky, which was reddening before my eyes. A few scattered clouds were hemmed with gold.

On a whim we decided to get out a few streets before the Opéra, so that we could walk a little before the concert. The driver stopped at a traffic light. We got out quickly, I took Kati by the arm, and we walked down one of the streets. As we were approaching the Place de la Bastille, someone whistled after us – a young fellow with ruffled straw-blond hair wearing shorts and a half-buttoned checked shirt. He winked at Kati, and inclined his head at a hat that lay on the ground by his feet, in which he had gathered a few coins. He raised his harmonica to his lips, played two or three bars, and began rhythmically nodding his head at us. Kati turned to me, laid her hand on my shoulder, pressed her stomach against mine . . . and . . . one-two-three . . . we began to dance, Kati and I, we began to dance on the pavement near the Place de la Bastille to the sound of a dissonant harmonica, to the one-two-three of a dissonant waltz, among the flickering headlights of passing cars, their rumbling engines, and the smiles on our faces, our bright eyes . . . Kati's long dress swished between our legs. Some passers-by swore at us.

If I could tear from my memory everything that happened after that short spontaneous dance, our first and our last, I would do so exactly as one might tear a few pages from a book. I would keep Kati's sudden effervescent laughter, and our holding hands as the coins tumbled into the hat of the blond young man with the harmonica, our breathlessness as we crossed the *place* and approached the square in front of the Opéra, the door that swung shut behind us, the stairs we climbed, the seats we sat in, still side by side, and how I felt her bare shoulder touching the cloth of my jacket. I would also keep Kati's bald-headed neighbour, whose eyes surreptitiously devoured her décolleté. I would keep the first part of the concert, Brahms's love songs, the intermission, our walk through the halls of the Opéra and the eyes following us – Kati, obviously, but also me. Her father? Lover? Husband? Friend? Teacher? people whispered. I would also keep the second part of the concert, the *Fourth Symphony* and the *Tragic Overture*, also by the challenging Herr Brahms. And the avalanche of fervour and enthusiasm that engulfed Simon after the few seconds of silence that followed the final chord. And his tortured, impenetrable face in the glare of the lights, his protracted gaze into the auditorium. Even Kati's stunned awe in the presence of this man. Even her hands, which she convulsively rubbed together – the most tangible sign of her anxiety.

But memory, according to Farkas, is not a dusty book from which one can tear at will such pages as one might deem unfortunate. If that were the case, we would have wings and be soaring through the clouds. And if that were the case – again, according to Farkas – I would never have met Kati-Katarina-Grushenka.

53

After the concert we were invited to the foyer: a glass of champagne, the usual superficial chitchat, head-nodding to the right and to the left, fixed smiles on lips. The rules of the game, as Simon and I had always given each other to understand with a quick glance. A wink from across the room: leopards, martens, squirrels . . . Kati and I walked down three flights of stairs. She remained enraptured. She walked as if in a trance, her eyes fixed in front of her. The halls were packed and it was not the best moment for an exchange of impressions and opinions. We had walked down the first flight of stairs, then the second and a third, and then I lost her: suddenly she was no longer next to me. I turned to the right, to the left, I stood on tiptoe, searching for something grass-green among the sea of dark silhouettes. I even called out her name, and a woman behind me snapped that this was the Opéra and not a sports arena. Perhaps she is waiting for me in the mezzanine. No. Perhaps on the ground floor. No. The crowd was streaming out of the main entrance. I wove my way through the back of the crowd from one side of the Opéra to the other. She had to be somewhere. Outside the main door, no doubt – perhaps she is waiting for me by the main door. I was holding her short velvet coat with the sparkling buttons. No, she wouldn't be waiting for me outside. She would be too cold in that thin dress. We had lost each other somewhere in the mezzanine. I went up to the first mezzanine. The second. I even looked inside the auditorium. I returned to the ground floor, which was now almost empty. Two young homosexuals with bleached hair asked if I had lost something and did I need help. I went out into the square in front of the Opéra. I searched among the people who stood about chatting. I went back inside, but was stopped from going upstairs. We're closing. I went back down to the ground floor, now completely empty, and took the lift to the terrace where the foyer was. An effervescent group of guests came pouring out into the hall. I made my way through them, looking to see if Kati was among them. "Excuse me, have you seen Simon Osterman?" I asked. Some shook their heads, others acted as if they had not heard me, or rather as if the question had not been directed to them. I noticed a dark man with tousled black hair, slightly hunched the way Simon always was after a concert. He turned his back on me and began talking to a buxom young woman. I made my way over to him and tapped him on the shoulder – it was not Simon.

"Do you know where I can find Simon Osterman?"

"Simon left immediately after the concert," he replied.

Simon left immediately after the concert . . . And Kati disappeared immediately after the concert . . . I took the lift back down to the ground floor. I was feeling increasingly feverish. Some sort of motorcycle gang seemed to have gathered in front of the Opéra. I roamed among their dark leather jackets and the icy sparkle of their motorbikes like a man lost in a strange forest among strange tree trunks. I gazed at these adventurous figures, at their cold faces, and tried to make my way through them, clutching Kati's coat to me. When I finally managed to break out of the circle I hailed the first free taxi driving past the *place*.

"Quai Voltaire, right by the bridge," I said. "I'm in a hurry, if you don't mind."

The driver scowled darkly into his mirror.

"You think I've got wings or something?"

"No, unfortunately you don't," I muttered under my breath.

54

Kati and Simon, I am convinced, also jumped into the first taxi at hand. Kati, of course, was feeling cold. Quai Voltaire, Simon had said, right by the bridge, as quickly as you can, he had added. The driver shot him a dark look in his mirror, and Simon regretted his words, since he had already placed his hand on Kati's thigh . . . His large, insistent hand, which slowly and methodically crept to the top, or rather, the beginning of her thigh . . . as he suddenly realized – there are always some things a man realizes too late – that a nocturnal drive through Paris is a far more exquisite form of foreplay than he had imagined.

I huddled in the corner of my taxi, almost pressing against the door, my eyes half-shut. Had I opened them, I would have seen Simon's hand on Kati's leg. Had I closed them, I would have seen his hand even more clearly creeping towards the inside of Kati's thigh. With my eyes half-shut, the world around me was blurred. The lights were distorted and poured like watercolours over my field of vision. Red, green, yellow drops sprayed over the blackness of the night. The buildings of the rue de Rivoli arched menacingly over me. The sky was visibly descending. The clouds and I gazed at each other. Finally the Seine calmed me a little.

"Which bridge?" the taxi driver asked.

Which bridge? I felt my heart tighten.

"That one there," I said, pointing.

I was no longer in such a hurry.

"No, it's that one over there," I said, pointing at the next bridge.

The driver heaved a loud sigh.

At the bridge I had to open my eyes in order to get some money from my pocket.

The driver wished me good night.

I walked back along the Seine to the corner of the rue du Bac. When I raised my eyes to the second floor of the corner building, to the flat which looks out onto the Seine, I felt a pain in my chest. The lights were out. They are probably in Simon's bedroom, I thought, and pushed open the heavy door and went through the lobby and into the courtyard. On this side too the lights of his flat were out. They've lit candles. I climbed the stairs. I rang. Once. Twice. Four times. Five times. Ten times. Are you going to open the door or not! Kati would open the door for me. Kati knows that I worry about her. Kati wouldn't leave me standing outside.

"What do you think you're doing? You'll wake up the whole building! Can't you see no one's in!" came an irate voice from behind the neighbour's door.

No one's in?

It was quite possible that the neighbour's voice was right – they hadn't come back here. They were not making love in the dark or by flickering candlelight. They had gone to the nearest hotel – the Hôtel Aurora, the Hôtel Idéal, the Conte – the first hotel they could find. Why hadn't I thought of this earlier?

"Thank you, thank you," I whispered back to the neighbour's voice and descended the stairs. Sometimes I truly lack imagination. After all, Kati is extremely hot-blooded. I had felt right from the start that fire flowed through those delicate, velvety veins of hers. After all, Kati knows what she wants. Kati, like Silvia, is prepared to make love anywhere. Beneath the shower, for instance. No! Not beneath the shower! Beneath the shower she and I had made love! On the carpet, on the carpet in the hotel room. On the wobbly table of the same hotel room. In the armchair . . . Against the door . . . Her dress, the colour of burnt grass, is lying discarded on the floor. One shoe on the bed, the other God only knows where . . . Simon, the conductor, the black bird, is no longer searching for detours, barriers, blind alleys, and other decelerations of rhythm. The outpour, O the momentous outpour is now inevitable. And now they are finally there, my sweet little girl, my joy. Now *we* are finally here, a smarting pang in my breast told me.

55

After trudging to the Hôtel Aurora, the Idéal, and the Conte, in which no Simon Osterman and companion had registered, and after the lone walk over the bridge and along the riverbank, and finally the taxi ride to number 73 Street of Disillusionment, the stairs to the fifth floor seemed never-ending. By the fourth floor I felt that the ascent to the fifth was a journey I would not be able to complete.

When I did manage it and, relieved, slid my key into the lock, I realized that the door was open. I remember that though I was surprised, I was not particularly unsettled; that I hung my jacket in the hall and put away Kati's short coat with the sparkling buttons. And that at the very moment I closed the armoire, I heard music. Yes, I heard somebody playing the piano. I remember that I stopped and hazily wondered who could possibly be playing; that I walked through my study towards the room with the piano from which the melodious sounds were coming. I even wondered whether it was Schumann, Brahms . . . or perhaps Schubert. And that I even leaned my head against the door, while the melody unstoppably drew nearer.

When I opened the door, I saw Simon and Kati before me.

I remember this lightning scene in all its clarity, as if it just unfurled before my eyes. A few steps away, at my black concert grand, Kati and Simon are sitting. Yes, it is no illusion, Kati and Simon. For a second I do not understand. How can they have come from the Hôtel Aurora, the Idéal or the Conte to the Street of Illusions? Where is the Schubert and the Schumann coming from? And the wineglasses on the piano, and Kati's red jacket over her light-green dress? Then I lean against the wall and no longer try to understand. I look at them, sitting side by side, so close that their shoulders are touching and Simon's wrists brush against Kati's. Finally I see them before me. That man who I chose for a friend, and that woman who in my mind I had also chosen . . . An attractive couple? An attractive couple. Definitely. No doubt about it, though it is like a sip of sugary liquid in my throat that I cannot, simply cannot, swallow. Their hands flow lightly over the keys. Kati is playing the melody, seriously, concentrated. Simon is accompanying her, very amicably, very amicably indeed. One would think they were playing for me alone, the sole listener in this vast night. That the night was deep, that the night was lively, that the night was light . . . perhaps . . . But then why do I feel a burning in my chest? Why is the wall behind me imperceptibly receding? Why is everything slowing down? Kati turns for a moment towards me, her face becomes more serious, silent.

"Tibor, we've been waiting for you since . . ." I managed to hear her say.

The bees come rushing towards me, an unknown swarm, a terrifying cloud, and I cannot hear anything except for their deafening buzzing . . . And all I see is Kati, leaving the piano, her face bending over me, flushed and sweet as it had been at the Hôtel Mon Rêve. After that I remember nothing.

56

"Did I not tell you to take care of yourself, you son of a lion? Do you think that a hospital room is the best place for a chat? Just look around you, if you please. Is that metal box with the lock on it supposed to be an armoire? And is that shed with its white coat of paint and its plastic shower and its plastic toilet bowl supposed to be a bathroom? And is this object next to your bed supposed to be a nightstand? Not to mention the print hanging above your head. A reproduction of a tapestry by an unknown weaver of the seventeenth century entitled 'Amor and Psyche' – that's what it says. What did you do, you son of a lion, for them to put you beneath a lake like that with a naked Psyche on its banks? Though I will admit that you frightened me. Tibor in the Bizet Clinic in the rue Bizet. Bizet as in Carmen. A heart attack, a minor one. But a heart attack, emergency room, peace and quiet, lots of it, and rest – is what the doctor on duty told me. Whatever you do, don't upset him, the doctor told me at least three times. Me? Why should I upset you?"

His yellow, fox-like eyes twinkled at me and he unbuttoned his jacket, beneath which he was wearing a patterned waistcoat with wooden buttons.

No, he wasn't upsetting me. I knew him and his fear of silence far too well. O sweet *horror vacui*! After two days of whispering doctors and the shuffling steps of nurses in the hallways, Farkas's warm baritone was a veritable relief. Even though I still had that strange feeling that my body was not my own, and that I was feeling a pain in someone else's chest. I was exhausted and weak, but that morning I had even managed with some difficulty to exchange a few words with Doctor Benjamin.

"I wanted to see you, you son of a lion! You know what I mean – one worries. The doe too . . . Grushenka . . . Kati."

I nodded. He had finally pronounced her name.

"She wanted to come instead of me. I had quite a hard time talking her out of it. Tibor, you son of a lion, I know this isn't the best time . . . but, well . . . about her . . . I maybe should have told you this earlier . . . right from the start. Do you remember that party I threw for Kaminsky?"

What was he talking about? Which Kaminsky?

"The author of *The Poisoning*."

The Poisoning?

"The fellow with the glasses – do you remember? The cocktail party at my place. I know I should have told you. But I didn't think that things would turn out the way they did between you, I really didn't. It never even occurred to me, you son of a lion."

I shook my head, and for a moment looked out of the window at the building across the way and a tree that was battling the wind.

"If I had known that you were intending to marry her just like that, right on the very first day, without mentioning a word to me . . . I still don't understand what got into you. Though I suppose the marriage didn't basically change things, did it? No, she had other plans."

"What are you talking about, Farkas?" I forced out.

"Are you telling me you never realized that Grushenka and I knew each other?" he asked, his voice changing abruptly.

I gazed at the spiral pattern of his waistcoat. Why was he telling me all this?

"One Monday morning, at the beginning of April, right in the middle of a sudden downpour, she came over to my office. I have no idea how she got past my secretary. She sat down in the armchair by the round table and took off her wet jacket. She told me that she'd like to meet you. That it was important for her. That it was urgent, imperative. That I had to help her. Yes, to help her, is what she said. As you know, I don't make a habit of handing out your phone number to any woman who asks me. She was quite calm and determined.

And soaked to the skin. I walked her to the stairs. At the door I told her that she could come to the cocktail party I was throwing for Kaminsky, and that she could meet you there. She kissed me on the cheek! Yes, even I was taken aback. I took her down to the courtyard, where a young man was waiting for her."

A man?

"'My brother,' she said, as she introduced him to me. But who knows. Because, you see, later on, during the summer, I ran into him in the café across the street. And as I'm not like you, you son of a lion, well, I went right up to him and asked him how his sister was. 'My sister?' he asked, and started laughing. 'Not my sister, nor my half-sister either!' It turns out that Grushenka has no family except for her mother, who lived for a few years with that fellow's father. Her father left them when she was twelve years old, he told me. Just disappeared without a trace. But Grushenka will be Grushenka – that was all he said. Grushenka will be Grushenka. I couldn't get anything else out of him, except that he's some sort of yoga teacher."

"Yoga?" I wheezed.

"Listen, you son of a lion. I know this isn't the right time. But I know that . . . Kati . . . has a deep affection for you . . . But that because of her . . ."

I waved my hand. Farkas fell silent for a moment. He took a handkerchief out of his pocket and mopped his brow.

"Tibor, you son of a lion . . ."

How strange, how very strange. This was the first time since I met Farkas, or rather, the first time since he has weighed me down with that "son of a lion" nickname which I have never managed to shake off, that the reason for this nickname dawned on me. Like an adult who suddenly discovers the meaning of a word that he kept repeating as a child without knowing what it meant. At that moment I realized that it was I and not Farkas who was the weaker in our rapport. That he is the lion, and that I am only his pitiful son.

"I don't know what game she's played with you or what she wanted," Farkas continued. "But what remains is that, basically, she played the game all the way."

I closed my eyes. The darkness behind my eyelids was – yes, yes – it was a bluish violet.

I wanted to rest, to think about something else. About anything, about the autumn that was coming to an end, about the plantain tree in the Rothschild park which by now must have lost all its leaves, and about the snot-nosed child whose mother had fallen asleep, her face pointing up to the sky.

57

"Yes, the autumn is coming to an end, the nights are getting longer, and the sky is clear and magnificent like in midsummer, so that one has the impression that one could see a star being born. Like the Chinese astrologer who in 1054, on the night of July 3 noticed a new, unusually brilliant star. The following morning he hurried with the news to the emperor. The new star brings us a promise of rich harvests, he proclaimed. And the people prepared a grand feast to celebrate the new star, which they named the Visitor. They made paintings of it and composed songs. But the star grew paler and paler, until a few nights later it disappeared completely," Eli Benjamin said, smiling at me with his slanted eyes.

What is the point of dwelling on what both of us know well enough: cardiac, cardinal, and so on. The tale of the visitor star's death – for the astrologer did not witness its birth, but its death – makes for perfect hospital-bedside chitchat. All doctors should also be astrophysicists, or, as my Agathe puts it, "What exists here exists elsewhere too."

"I'll check on you again tomorrow morning," Eli Benjamin said, and left my room.

"There's someone waiting for you outside," he said, his head popping back in through the door. "Your . . ."

She came in a few moments later. I heard her exchange a few words with him.

She closed the door behind her and leaned against it. She was breathing through her mouth, taking short, laboured breaths. She was wearing her black velvet coat, and her red heart-shaped bag hung on her arm. Her face was washed-out, almost translucent. We stared at one another as if we had returned from far away. As if we were standing on the platform of a train station, I suddenly thought. She and I. That young woman with blonde hair that was finally covering her forehead and was again beginning to curl into ringlets by her temples, with honey-coloured skin, with the delicate scar above her eyebrow, with her wide lips that gave one the impression they were floating in her face.

And he, visibly worn out, trembling with weakness and anxiety, though he is trying hard to hide that he is trembling. Her clothes, the black velvet coat with the sparkling buttons, and that red heart – how can it be that I did not think of it right away – are like a sign between them.

The train is about to leave and they still have not said anything definite.

"Grushenka!" I suddenly call out, and right away realize that I have never before pronounced that name. Never, not even that first evening in the taxi.

"Grushenka!" I repeat with difficulty, as though I am trying to accustom myself to it.

She moves, shudders, as though I had just brushed her with a whip, as though I had uttered the one word she had least expected to hear, the one word she had not braced herself for. She hides her hands in her pockets, her red bag slips down to her wrist. I have the impression that she has suddenly become paler beneath her pallor.

"Kati," she corrects me hesitantly.

"It's Kati, Tibor," she repeats, stubborn, imploring, commanding.

"What is it she wants from me?" flashes through my mind. "What is it you want from me?" I would like to force out of my throat. "Tell me what?" I want her to tell me once and for all. Right now, in this room, with her back against the door, with that ridiculous red thing, which belongs in the nearest dustbin, hanging from her wrist. In a few words, once and for all.

Suddenly a sharp ray of early winter sun creeps into the room and brushes her face as if it wanted to slap her, and she closes her eyes and turns away.

"Kati!" I recognize my voice.

Two, three steps and she is at the side of my bed.

"Make some space for me," she orders, as if she were suddenly in an incredible hurry.

Before I even manage to move, she lies down next to me in her coat, her bag in her hand, and nestles her head close to mine, and, just as during the night of her fever, I feel her skin, her hair, her breath against my body. If I had enough strength I would pull her onto me and would clench her in a tight embrace, I think to myself. I try to move, to raise my head or at least the arm next to which she is lying.

"The piano . . . Why did you tell me you didn't know how to play the piano?" I heard myself say.

"Shh," she whispered into my ear and laid her hand on my mouth. "Shh."

What cold hands she has! Her extremities are always cold. That was why she had worn gloves in the middle of April.

Then suddenly she gets out of bed. She rearranges her coat and her hair.

"Doctor Benjamin is waiting for me outside. Just a few minutes, he told me. Just a few minutes, and not a word," she murmurs, picking up her bag which had fallen on the floor. By the door she turns and looks at me once more, and quickly, hurriedly, raises her hand in farewell.

58

The brief premonition of a farewell on the platform of a railway station when she visited me at the Bizet Clinic became reality much faster than I could have imagined, though there was no platform, no railway station, and ultimately no farewell.

A few long days after Kati's visit, Eli Benjamin drove me

back to the rue Balzac in his car. With the approval of his colleagues he had arranged for my discharge from the clinic, after I gave him my solemn word that I would adhere strictly to his instructions.

"I will take you up to the flat," he said, leaning over to the back seat for my bag.

"But only as far as the door," I answered, and got out of the car.

We climbed the stairs slowly, taking long rest periods on each floor.

"Are you sure you don't want someone to stay with you?" he insisted when we finally reached my front door on the fifth floor.

"I'm sure," I said with a quick nod, looking straight in front of me, though I could just as well have shaken my head. Never before had I needed someone so badly. That was why I wanted to go back home alone. I wanted to open the door, walk over to her, put down my bag, here I am, back home, back at our place, I wanted to sense her smell upon me, sit in our corner on the Anatolian carpet or at the kitchen table, or on the sofa, take both her hands in mine, gaze at her. And then discuss things. Not necessarily in order, her visit to Farkas, her brother who was not her brother, and whom I had seen that night in her wrought-iron bed, the piano, good God, why had she told me that she did not know how to play the piano? But to talk openly, eye to eye, like that ray of sunlight that had blinded her for an instant.

"Call me any time, even at night."

I continued looking straight in front of me and waited for Eli Benjamin to leave.

"As you know, I always enjoy talking with you," he continued in a confiding tone, as though he had no intention of leaving, as if his words were merely a prelude to a conversation about stars and people. But he finally did give me his narrow, bony hand, and went down the stairs.

I waited for his footsteps to fade away on the lower floors, and unlocked the door. I wiped my sweating hands on my trousers and walked into the hall.

The flat smelled clean and inert. The balcony door in my study was open. The kitchen tidy. In the fridge, fresh milk, bread, a few slices of cheese. On the table, the post and a basket of fruit. All traces of the last concert had disappeared from the room with the piano. The Anatolian carpet corner, desolate, abandoned.

I walked past my untouched room and opened the door of the semicircular room with the cupola. I gasped. It was empty. Empty. Nothing on the floor. Nothing on the table either. The bed was covered with the pink bedspread that Marie-Hélène had left behind. All that was left was the spindly plant, the one without roots, standing on the chest of drawers by the door. It had grown so much that it was almost hanging down to the floor.

I opened the door and went out onto the arterial balcony. The early afternoon was bathed in the same silvery-pale sunlight that had dazzled Kati's eyes a few days before. The sky was high and clean, with a few ragged clouds here and there. I could see from a distance that the gates of the Rothschild park were locked. The trees below me, now leafless, threw their long shadows over the pavement.

I sat down at my desk and picked up the telephone. I dialled

Eli Benjamin's number. I heard his slightly shrill voice: "You have dialled the number of Doctor Eli Benjamin. If your call is urgent, or you wish me to call you back when I return, please leave a message after the three beeps."

I waited for the three short beeps. I had to tell someone.

"Hello . . . this is Tibor. My heart is aching, Doctor Benjamin . . . Kati has left me."

59

I would be lying if I were to say that I did not wait for her to come back. Just as I would be lying if I were to say that I did not try to reconstruct Kati's and my story, including Farkas's assertions, in other words Kati's coming to his office, and the man with the closely cropped hair and the silver ring who was waiting for her among the Greek columns, who by all accounts was neither her brother nor her half-brother, even though some years back they had lived beneath the same roof during a period when Kati's mother was living with his father. Or if I said that I did not try to imagine her vagabonding years when she was young, in which she seems to have learnt all those languages, or her separation from her father who left her mother and her, Kati-Katarina-Grushenka, before she was even twelve years old, probably never getting over his betrayal of her. Or if I said that I did not weigh up Farkas's assertions that she had led me by the nose, tricked me, played some kind of charade, sham, or farce, which could so easily have turned into a tragedy, and – a round of applause for Mademoiselle – that she played her role with true talent, managing even to rope in a real-life orchestra conductor, taking the baton out of his hand without his even noticing and conducting the whole score on her own. Or if I said that I did not think that in some way, perhaps well before the overture, Farkas had been mixed up in all of this, for he has been hounding me for some years now to write a romance novel, or if I said that I did not continue unravelling Kati's and my story, from the beginning, from the back room of one of the restaurants I used to go to, the little wet boat on the white Burgundy bumping into the wall of the glass, to her embrace at the Bizet Clinic and her hurried goodbye, raising her hand as if she were standing in the door of a departing train.

Every day I waited for her. Every morning at the same time I sat down at my desk, spreading out all manner of notes, turned on my typewriter, and typed a few sentences, at times even a whole page. At about ten, I slowly sipped a cup of coffee, my only cup of coffee all day, and continued typing my sentences. After all, I had to find something to do until noon. She might drop by at noon for lunch, unexpectedly, as is her nature. I fixed us a little something to eat. After lunch, I would lie down on the sofa in the kitchen, and usually fell into a short, deep sleep, very much like the one she had awakened me from on the afternoon she had cut her hair. After my siesta I had a new habit, which turned out to be both pleasant and also extremely good for my heart: a walk through the Rothschild park. I would sit down on a bench not far from the entrance to the museum and stare before me. As it was early winter, the park was almost deserted, and Manuel's hens and cockerels were already rambling among the bushes and in the hollow between the trees. The leaves had been raked together into a big pile. My tall plantain tree, the tallest in the park, was as bare as old age. When I got back home, I started to become anxious. She usually came home around this time. I lit a cigarette, one of the five that Eli Benjamin allowed, and sat down in the armchair that stood between the fireplace and the window. I pricked up my ears – would there be a clicking in the lock, would her footsteps echo in the hall, would the door open surreptitiously and her head suddenly appear? I gazed at my piece of sky, at the approaching evening, at my favourite time of day, now departing . . . And yet I was ready at any moment to turn around to her and open my arms.

I waited for her at night. From two until three, or possibly three-thirty . . . the hours of my darkest ravine. When the last streetlamp went out in the neighbouring avenue, when I no longer heard the footsteps of some nocturnal pedestrian, my only brother, I crossed the arterial balcony and went to the semicircular room with the cupola. I opened the door as quietly as I could and sat down on the wrought-iron bed. I gazed at it for a long time. Until my eyes began to burn. Until the night began to thin.

And until one of these nights, when she will rise out of the darkness. Kati-Katarina-Grushenka. Curled up, her arm clamped around one shoulder, her face half-hidden by her hair . . . That body, that I once held upon me . . . Her undulating breath . . . And even – yes, yes – her talking in her sleep. In that unknown tongue which, after all our nights together, I feel is almost part of me . . . Definitely part of me . . . My God, I listened to her words and for the first time in my life sensed something clear, simple, and plain-spoken, which until now I had never managed to attain.

"What a charade, sham, or even tragedy," she said. "But let us call it theatre, if we really have to call it something. We know that we are appearing on the same stage – though in different roles, different plays. Only that mostly we do not choose them, we simply happen to come upon them. The roles of father, lover, daughter . . ."

She suddenly fell silent, as if something had caught in her throat. I bent down closer to her.

"It was I who chose you, Tibor," she continued almost in a whisper. "Just as you chose me. Only that I chose you first. I knew everything about you, from the words hidden behind the R. and the A., to Ema and her affair with Manuel, to the names of your two lunchtime restaurants. By the way, did you never ask yourself how it was that I knew where to find you that day in your restaurant near the boulevard Saint-Germain, the restaurant in which you asked for my hand in marriage? For my hand, mine, while all I wanted was to be your daughter. Don't look so surprised! Why should I not be allowed to choose a father? I wanted someone to look after me. Yes, you. I wanted you to wait for me to come home. To look after me when I was sick . . . To choose glasses for me. My new glasses . . . To worry about me, be angry with me, to despair of me. Even to be jealous. Like all fathers. Only you crossed all the boundaries of jealousy. I did try to help you, to give you little signs – 'Children will be children' – remember? The rue Jules Verne, the Seven Wonders Café? But I thought, how shall I put it, well, that you'd be more clear-sighted. Don't be angry with me, Tibor . . ."

Again she swallowed, and then continued in a lower voice,

so that I had to bend down even closer to read the words from her lips.

"What you could say is, we chose the same play – *Love* – but not the same roles, and that we played them . . . with *brio*, you must admit. Yes, precisely, *con brio*. Say it, Tibor, you do agree, don't you?"

60

"Excuse me, would you mind moving over one seat? I would like to sit by the window."

"No, I'm sorry," I told the young woman in a checked jacket and thick glasses that made her large eyes even larger. "This is my seat."

She stared at me, as did the two other passengers sitting in the first four seats behind the driver on bus number 31.

This is, after all, my seat, and the bus is my laboratory. Number 31, Place de l'Étoile–Gare du Nord, the first window seat behind the driver. In the bus my thoughts are at their lightest and most daring, I would tell people who were surprised at this habit of mine. I sit and watch . . . as if I were sitting in a sunlit cinema. And slowly my thoughts are awakened, corralled, and then, indomitable, begin to roam free. Those faces, the young woman with the thick glasses and the checked jacket, the elderly man with the Daliesque moustache, the baby in the back of the bus babbling away happily, a blonde, who turns her back to me – that narrow street with the exotic merchandise, where outlandish tubers and green bananas are sold, and then that sky, already touched by spring –

everything is like a springboard to new combinations.

"Well then, go and ride that bus of yours, you son of a lion," Farkas said to me. "Spring will be here any day now," he mumbled, allowing for a few moments of silence, as he always does when he begins to despair about me.

"It's true, spring will be here any day now," I echoed, and added that I was aware of the situation and so, for financial reasons, had started work on a new novel. A novel about the mysterious death of an opera singer, I said.

And why not, I thought, eyeing the short-sighted woman sitting next to me, trying to imagine my new prima donna who would have to die. A blonde? No. No. Dark-haired? Or a redhead, like Baleli, or that other lady, or the young woman with the chiselled profile and the short fiery hair who is leaning her head against the window, staring ahead just like I am? Anyway, opera singers always wear wigs.

The bus filled up, as it always does on this long street. The woman with the thick glasses next to me got up and began making her way towards the door. I followed her with my eyes. Not far from her, by the exit, stood another woman holding onto the metal bar. I got up so I could see her better. I made my way over towards her.

"Excuse me, excuse me," I said, pushing my way through the crowd. She had blonde hair that barely covered her ears. The broad shoulders of a swimmer, long forearms that peered out from the rolled-up sleeves of her short blue blouse. For a second I managed to see her profile, high cheekbones, a straight nose.

"Excuse me, excuse me."

Her hand, holding onto the metal bar – a slim, strong, bony

hand – loosened its grip, moved.

"Kati!" I shouted.

She stepped off the bus and the clattering door fell shut behind her.

"Kati! Kati!" I shouted after her, though the bus had begun to move again. I watched her walk away through the crowd, stop by the traffic light, wait for it to turn green, and disappear into the first street that crossed the thoroughfare.

Perhaps it wasn't Kati I said to myself, sitting down again in my seat behind the driver and looking at the pale-blue sky, which was beginning to darken. If it had been Kati, she would surely have heard me. Even though the door had clattered, drowning out my voice. If it had been Kati she would have turned around. She would have waved, even if only hurriedly and with a half-raised hand, as she did at the Bizet Clinic or at the Italian restaurant in the avenue Lord Byron. Be that as it may, we will definitely meet again. Paris is our town, my sweet Slovenian girl.